ACCREDITATION TIME

Harvey Price

Publisher: Harvey L. Price, Jr.
Madras, Oregon

ISBN: 978-0-9819220-5-8

Library of Congress Control Number: 2010900946

Back cover: "Lost World". Image used with permission and purchased through http://www.dreamstime.com.

Front cover: Weatherwax, Ocean Shores, Washington. Photo taken by author- 2009.

CentralPark.com Runner's Map: Used courtesy of CentralPark.com.

Subway and bus maps © Metropolitan Transportation Authority. Used with permission.

Printed by Minuteman Press, Olympia, Washington, and bound by Phil's Bindery, Seattle, Washington.

FOR

ALL THE KEEPERS, DOERS AND PEOPLE
OF GOOD WILL WHO WORK
TIRELESSLY FOR A BETTER DAY AND FOR
OUR NEXT ACCREDITATION
SURVEY

Also written by Harvey Price

ACKNOWLEDGEMENT

Special recognition should be given to the Joint Commission for the Accreditation of Health Care Organizations. Having had to prepare for several of their surveys, I can hardly imagine the difficulty Eve and Adam would have had surveying our entire world, even if it was condensed down to performing it solely in Manhattan.

Likewise, I want to again give eternal thanks to Jeannie, who is ever-patient and long-suffering throughout my battles with the written word. She embodies, for me, what it means to be a true artist; her canvas being life itself. Even as the shades are lowered further for her, her courage and love are true and boundless.

And as always, Tom and Elizabeth Hicker have given this book their customary, energetic review and desperately needed editing. Any omissions or mistakes found now are solely mine. They have struggled to show me the best way to present this material. Their patience is the stuff of legends.

And finally, to Adam and Eve, wherever they may be, I am truly grateful to them for the part they may have played in making it possible for me and all of you to experience the wonder of life.

FOREWORD

Bringing Adam and Eve back to our shores was not an easy undertaking. Luckily for Eve, but not so much for Adam, this accreditation survey was to be their last. Much has been asked of them, and certainly they deserve a well-earned rest when this final survey is completed. Their using Manhattan as the microcosm for our entire world was probably done to save them some travel time. I could think of no finer place to choose than New York City.

THE RETURN

ONE: SOME CLARIFICATION

Probably, before we get too far into this tale of inspection, discovery and self-revelation, I need to tell you that our first venture onto this world was also my very first anywhere. And because I stayed here until I was 930 years old, if you can believe that, you have to try and accept that other, even more amazing events have occurred for Eve and I since that rather delayed departure.

Also, I need to inform you that what I am about to tell you was something that I am attempting to record on a daily basis. Over time I've discovered that was the only way I can remember what happened on any given day. To wait more than one day after something occurred meant that it never did...at least in my mind. You're just going to have to cut me some slack here. After all, my being well over 550,000 years old, should entitle me to a little respect; I'm well into my "senior years", according to anyone's calendar.

However, on second thought, just mentioning what my age is on the end of my first stay here brings up a minor, but to me, a puzzling question. If I was destined to live that long on your world, why couldn't it have been just seventy years longer and rounded the total out to an even millennium. It would have made the bookkeeping work that was to follow later so much easier. Come to think of it, you most likely have no idea why I would care. But believe me, you will, once I get further into the reason I am back here now.

And to provide you a better grasp of my bona fides, before I get too much further into more of the details regarding my returning, let me say that those eons ago, upon my first appearance or emergence, if you will, EVERYTHING, and I mean EVERYTHING, was a shock and surprise to me. Why? Because I hadn't existed until then.

But you no doubt will reply, "So what's so stunning about that? None of us now alive nor any of our relatives or ancestors before us ever existed… until we were born. What makes you so special?"

Ah, hah! That's the one, true decisive difference between any and all of you out there and me. You were actually born, immediately began the trial and error learning process and then had reinforced all you know gradually over a period of many years. Me? I just suddenly appeared one day: full-grown, standing in the middle of leafy, tall things, surrounded by every kind of noise, coming from all manner of different creatures. And I was buck naked! There was no new-being-just-arrived orientation, remedial classes and homework, evening seminars, any mentors, other colleagues or companions to prepare or to guide me. What I arrived with that first day was all I had going forward. Just put yourselves in my shoes, which didn't even exist yet.

Now, don't get me wrong. Bemoaning my humble beginnings isn't my way of trying to excuse the mistakes I made in the days and weeks after my first appearance here. A guy does what he does. Sometimes we think ahead. Most often, however, we just do; thinking ahead creates confusion and seems to lead to complications. And even after all these countless years, I'm more often than not forging ahead first, letting any rational thoughts follow. I suppose it's a guy thing.

But, again, don't get me wrong. I'd like to be brilliant and clever; it might have before, and even now, reduced my decision-to-error ratio. Probably the Original Plan for me was to arrive on-scene as a mature, stable, logically thinking and acting individual. Well, it didn't happen. I bumble along and always have... and probably always will. I do have my good moments, and then I hope that all's forgiven. After they occur, I begin to think that now I'll cruise along knowing in advance or at the appropriate time exactly what to think, say or do. But they are brief and fleeting.

Having said this, try putting yourself in my

shoes, sandals, or as it really was, in my bare feet; obviously, I would have no idea what foot-ware looked like in those initial moments of my being launched. And now attempt to grasp, at least a smidgen of my bewilderment. Add to all my confusion, I was beginning to shiver. Everything else around me was wearing bark, feathers, hair or fur. What was that all about?

I initially figured that my appearing like this had to be a test. There I was: alone, naked and absolutely dumbfounded as to where I was and WHY. I did have enough sense to appreciate that this was my dawning... my coming out, as it were. A little fanfare might have been appropriate; something to mark the occasion. But everything about me went on its merry way... ignoring me. I didn't even look tasty enough to eat. It was only after I eventually put on the silliest excuse for some clothes that I started being stalked. To figure out why then, you might ask, just look at yourself in a mirror sometime after you've just stepped out of the shower and see what I mean...

Well, anyway, upon my first arrival here, I stumbled around for a while, nibbling on this and that. It was sheer displacement activity on my part. I had never walked, run, sang or played a musical instrument. And in those first few days I would have really loved to know how to build a fire. I needed a break from the mounting stress during those earliest days. What guy doesn't feel better when he is sitting by a campfire...even if he's naked?

And so those lonely, first days passed with me somehow trudging around aimlessly. Possibly I may have muttered something out loud, but even that would have been fairly rudimentary and incoherent. Nothing else around me talked. So how was I supposed to just start carrying on a conversation? As I recall, it was also around this time I began to think, which again was, and I guess still is, pretty painful and surprising, that having someone in the neighborhood who at least resembled me would be nice. We could at least stare at each other, even if we couldn't talk.

And lo and behold, it was soon after I had this stray thought, sometime during a particularly world-altering night, a sobering and brazenly invasive procedure was performed on me. And let's be honest at the outset; I'm almost certain what happened that night would most likely have surprised you as well.

After I awoke that next morning, I had a heck of a pain in my left chest wall. Someone or Something had taken the liberty to remove one of my RIBS! Now that really set me to worrying. What part of me would be next? There was no "May I" or "Do you Mind?" It just happened.

As I was attempting to recover somewhat from the shock of that intrusion, I looked up and standing beside me was a true vision. It was Eve. But of course at that point in our relationship, we hadn't given ourselves names yet. That came much later. But as I faintly recall, the process of giving names to ourselves all started with that silly palindrome you've probably heard about so often; the "Madam I'm Adam" one.

It actually just blurted out one day. What made me say "Adam" still baffles me. In those days I didn't say much, because I thought everything I said had to say should say the same thing when reversed. It's just the way my mind worked back then. Play it forward; then play it backward. And if it says the same thing, then you must mean it. That was my motto in those days. And it was a little later, about the time I happily expanded on that first announcement to Eve by saying, "Madam, in Eden, I'm Adam", that I caught her rolling her eyes and shaking her head.

"Can't you just talk to me, like a normal person?" she asked immediately thereafter, with a hint of frustration in her voice. "Surely, you've got more to say than that meaningless dribble."

And you know; she was right. But I've got to say that those earliest attempts by me to speak probably laid the foundation for men everywhere. We're just not the conversationalists others would want us to be. You guys out there come by your stony silence or monosyllabic responses naturally. I'm to blame. In those days it was a natural progression for me to eventually incorporate "uh huh," "yes, pet," "um, hum," "you bet," and "why not?" into my growing vocabulary. I consider it the first-ever examples of someone trying to be a conservationist.

But now I suppose it is time to mention something about that rather awkward incident involving the hanging fruit from the "Good Turned Evil Tree", as I came to call it. Maybe it's true that Eve had had some ongoing discussions with that sorry serpent, fellow just prior to that well-publicized decision of mine. However, the decision to take a bite out of that apple was mine alone. And I understand after that little mishap, Eve seemed to get the blunt of the blame. I regret that. I would have signed a confession, but I didn't know how to write yet.

So, ever since then, both of us have had to do some serious repair work to get out from behind The Creator's wood shed, so to speak. Believe me, when I had it to do over again, which as it turned out I did countless times, but never again on your world's premises, I had become a strict meat, mash potatoes and gravy-eating man. My days of sampling odd-bits of fruit had come to an end. Well, that's not absolutely correct. I still sneak in a fresh date or two every now and then. I mean, come on, dates were without question the very first fruit; and no date I've ever eaten claimed beforehand to know everything or the difference between right and wrong.

It's simply a small, tasty fruit produced by a very tall palm tree. The truth is they are nothing you should choose to eat haphazardly. Because to ensure you are eating them at their most delicious time, you have to climb about thirty feet up in the air to get the best ones. I just needed you to know. It's a holdover guilty feeling I get when discussing fruit. I can't be too cautious. Who knows, maybe one day dates will be off limits too.

But none of this fruit-eating business was Eve's fault, believe me. I'd been eying that juicy-looking, luxuriantly golden apple, hanging from the so-called "knowledge" tree for some time. And it's time I have that confession in print for all to see. One has to own up to his or her individual involvement in a matter as serious as this, if you ever want to put behind you a particularly sorry episode in your life. And honestly, it didn't even taste that good… it was too bitter. Ever after taking that bite, I often wondered what kind of knowledge that particular apple was supposed to represent. It would have been a real disappointment for someone looking for a brilliant breakthrough.

Honestly, even now I can't fully grasp what all the fuss is about. It has to have been a Creator Thing. If we were not supposed to eat anything from that tree, there should have been a sign hanging from it, saying: "DO NOT EAT FROM THIS TREE!!. HAZARDOUS TO YOUR FUTURE!! THIS MEANS YOU… ADAM!"

I mean, I was still trying to get my sea-legs when all this happened. I didn't even know yet what a "good" deed was, much less what all this "evil" business was about. But, I suppose, life comes at you from all directions. And sometimes the roadmap you've used for a particular day has no "beware" or "caution" signposts. Then, "Wham!" you're hit by a stupid, personal decision; an accident; disease or a sudden loss of a loved one. I've begun to think that as time goes by, everyone at some point has a chew or two on that same fruit; but now it's simply invisible. How fair is that?

Anyway, moving on, let me also say that way too much has been made about that subsequent fig leaf-business. Even I knew when I was naked before all that fruit-eating confusion arose! It didn't take eating some bitter-tasting, low-hanging apple to tell me that. I mean, come on… Maybe my interior lights don't glow too brightly nor do I reflect a radiance or aura of a learned scholar, but I knew full-well, immediately upon my arrival in this world, that my first stop needed to be to see a tailor.

So why did Eve and I have to sport those fig leaves? Have you ever tried wearing one? It's not like they come with belts or suspenders attached. And boy, does it ever look goofy to run around holding one in front of you. To me, that was punishment enough for whatever misdeed I had committed. You could hear all the animals and birds chuckling around us. Some even pointed at us as we tried to be inconspicuous.

And while I'm at it, one of my first acts as one of two of the founding members of the human race, on this our return visit to your world, is to proclaim that using "fowl" to describe the wondrous birds we met and knew in this world is archaic and prejudicial. It's like calling all animals "beasts" or all humans "creatures". We all need to respect and treat each other better. Labeling something or someone can lead to carelessness and unwarranted harm. No doubt you've seen enough of that already.

And yes, to move along in my review of those earlier times, Eve and I were evicted from Eden. Just the same, it wasn't like we'd been there that long to begin with. But it did seem like a nice place. It was more the circumstance surrounding our having to leave that was so embarrassing and painful. I've always liked to travel and see other places, so moving on wasn't that bad. Eve, however, took it pretty hard. You couldn't blame her. I was still talking in fits and starts, running words and sentences together and mumbling. Bless her heart; she thought at first it was because I was overwhelmed about our sudden eviction notice, which I must admit did hamper my progress some. But actually my talking more coherently was more a matter of simply learning how to put the necessary prepositions, adverbs, adjectives, spaces and pauses together properly. Eve has always been much better at that than me. Still is.

You can see what I mean by my giving you a rough example. Let's take the first day after we'd been shipped out of The Garden and what I attempted to say to calm Eve.

"Imreallysorrythatthishappenedwhateveryou rnameisandbythewaydidyounoticethatserpentfriendo fyour'sisnolongerwalkonlegswhoeverheardofasnake withoutlegs?!"

See what I mean? It drove her crazy.

So our first few days, once we were out of The Garden, were spent with her teaching me how to slow down, punctuate and try to think before I spoke. Try learning that in a few days! Punctuation and word separation came eventually, but thinking before speaking: THAT is THE CHALLENGE of a lifetime. And the reason for both of us returning here to your world at this time is, in part, to see how well you folks out there have managed that skill as well.

Well, time marched on for Eve and I. She eventually picked her own name, which I couldn't help but like, because it could be reversed and still be the same. She rolled her eyes again when I commented on how clever I thought it was on her part to choose it. Her doing so probably indicated that it was an oversight on her part; and if she could do it again, she'd choose "Josephine" or "Katherine".

Already, her selecting "Eve" gave me the feeling that we were going to be life-long buddies or pals. Marriage?... That was an entirely different matter. Why do you think we lived 930 years together our first assignment on your world? It took the better half of that time to bring myself to formally propose marriage. It wasn't like I was particularly shy. Commitment was a MAJOR issue... no; it's THE MAJOR issue for a guy; even if you like someone's name, and she lets you stay around her for over 450 years! So you gals out there; blame me for that personality disorder. It all started with me.

But eventually we did tie the little knot and produced our two sons: Cain and then Able. Tragically, there was all that terrible business between our two boys, and we were left with just the one. And as you are probably aware, after Eve and I had lived 130 years longer, she bore our third son, Seth. Now there's a surprise for you! Seth's mother and I had hardly just met, relatively speaking, and his two brothers came along; and then we waited another 128 years, and she gave birth to him. You can bet at that age there was no possibility of me playing baseball or beach volleyball with him after school or on the weekend.

But little did we know that we were just getting started with our time on this world; we had another 800 years to go!! If Guinness and company were looking for a record that can't be broken, there's one for them. And I do apologize to those of you out there who might find our living arrangement, having children and postponing marriage so long a concern. It wasn't like I was aware of all the social implications of those delays. Just remember; I'm slow.

Eve and I never again felt comfortable with our roles as parents, after losing Able. We tried to make amends with our rearing Seth, but each of you out there have probably already figured out that you do your best, hope and pray for the best, and then have to let your children make their own way. Some are early bloomers, some blossom in due time but, sadly for some, the much anticipated blooming never occurs. It's like what's been planted just doesn't manage to take root; no matter what is done. It's like they were planted during the wrong season, on untillable ground, with seeds that had lost their zest. Or possibly, it was too late in the season when the earliest shoots appeared, and they didn't have their full measure of nutrients early on in life. Whatever the reason or reasons, over and over again Eve and I worked tirelessly to nurture and encourage Seth. But we always worried and grieved. We still do.

Begging your pardon, if you will, please excuse another departure in my regaling you with a few past events of our first coming out in your world; but if you will, allow me just one more sober observation. What happened to Able left a void that Eve and I never filled. The death of a child, no matter her or his age, leaves a parent without any mooring lines. You are cast adrift. Sometimes you come in sight of land again, but ever-lurking are memories that push you away from the safety of peaceful rest and solace. It is a loss accompanied by incomparable sorrow. It leaves you clinging on to a sliver of hope that one day, in a realm far different from the harshness of this one; you will be reunited again, forevermore, with that child. From the moment of his death, all Eve and I could do was hold tightly onto each other until that day came. And, again, we still do.

Frankly, this is not the time, nor the place, to delve into the causes of Abel's death. But I'm sure by now there have been volumes written, discussing the events and circumstances that led up to that event or about Cain's rationalization for what he did. They were both our sons, for Pete's sake; and Eve and I have avoided pointing fingers or judging. We leave all that up to you who are scattered throughout the orbs of life, extending across this or any other Universe that there might be.

So that brings me back to my earlier use of the phrase: "… which I did countless times". What does that mean? In short, it's an acknowledgement and warning that Eve and I have gone through more time zones than there are clocks to record them. And we've traveled distances that there aren't enough zero's to measure them. But here's the catch: we didn't know until just before I began writing this, that we'd be returning to your world. Each time we started life anew on another world; events progressed similar to the way they did on our first attempt here. Much, much later, after we completed that first phase of The Very Grand Plan, we began the process of returning to each world for the second one. And, amazingly, we started returning to them in reverse chronological order that we departed them.. The last to leave became our first to revisit. You could say there has been no rest for the most weary.

"Then why hasn't Eve spoken up, if both of you have returned," you might ask. She will, believe me. It's just that she asked me to give you this brief introduction, while she rested a bit from our endless travels. My guess is that she probably had an inkling that something like this was inevitable, but she never let on to me. You see, our first experience here was our most traumatic and memorable. She has always tried to protect my rather fragile psyche ever after. And, in turn, I have tried to protect her from physical attack. Our returning to this world has both of us more nervous than usual. We fear something may go wrong again. Never fear though, you'll be hearing from her soon enough, I guarantee you.

And finally, you might ask, at least at the beginning of this strange and improbable reappearance of ours, if it is even remotely possible to believe any of this I have told you or that you have read about before, why in heaven's name have we returned? And please bear in mind that I have little or no memory of anything that we do in our previous stays on other worlds. That makes it easier for us to do the business that we are commissioned to do with each new assignment. All I really know is that we had to keep repeating our first assignment and then we had to begin another one in the reverse order. What exactly we've done each time escapes me. But probably not Eve.

However, saying that, from what I am very slowing beginning to comprehend, almost as if the full light of our multiple lifetimes of travail are coming into full focus; for the first time, we are here again in your midst to perform the duties of an Accreditation Committee. If you will, try to imagine for this, our return visit, to compare us to your JCAHO Review Body, the one which is charged with inspecting and approving continued operation of your hospitals and health care facilities nationwide. That's right; we're here to do an inspection. And it will be our final one. After it is completed, we have just been informed that we can retire for good. It's a prospect that gives Eve and I great comfort. You will have to admit that by all accounts, we must be nearing the age of retirement.

But now it's time to begin the inspection. As I understand it, this final one will be a little different from the thousands we have done previous to this. We will not be traveling from country to country, province to province or municipality to municipality. Instead, for this inspection we are staying entirely on the Island of Manhattan. It is to serve as the microcosm for your entire world. From all Eve and I have gathered, it is here in this small location that peoples from every corner of your world have migrated, settled and produced the most diverse and productive city on the planet. It is the cosmopolitan center of your world. And we are thrilled to be staying here for a brief time.

A final report on the state of your world and our recommendations and conclusions should accompany our inspection and findings. And I realize this all sounds so official, coming from someone who manages to bungle up the smallest chores and who is overwhelmed by the most modest of changes in his environment. That's why Eve is so precious. She understands me and gives me the helping hand that I need to survive and bungle through any assignment given me. All this said, after my, most likely, surprising introduction and a somewhat cursory explanation of our circumstances; let us now see how well you folks have been doing since Eve and I left you so long ago.

TWO: CENTRAL PARK

"A.J.!! WHERE ARE YOU?!!"

Hearing that, I knew Eve had awakened. Her nap time was over, and we needed to get started on this final leg of our seemingly endless journey. By the end of these next seven days, we will be FINALLY AND COMPLETELY DONE. All the life we had started throughout the Universe and all the return accreditation visits we had to perform will have been completed. The Creator has given us the Word that finally, following our initial mishap in Eden and after completing this final week's work; our eons-old, doghouse-days will be over. We'll be free at last to find a measure of eternal rest in The Creator's arms. Who could pass up a promise like that?

Both of us have been getting so excited over the last hour or so. To realize that we would be gathering information and making the evaluations on the one world we loved so very much and remembered the best of all. And to know we'll soon be able to share our findings with everyone, in a forum that will allow us to broadcast it to the world when we are finished. It is impossible right now to give you any inkling what we've anticipated discovering or what our recommendations, if any, might be. But they will be different from what we have told other worlds where we've both initiated life and then returned to do a follow-up assessment of its successes. This world, our very first, is our favorite; and it is the one we are most anxious to tell everyone here what we have found. We're anticipating it will be a glowing report. You can't know how proud we are to have been returned here for this honor. But, for now, you are just going to have to wait on what we have to say. Sorry. Consider it a Founding Mother and Father's prerogative.

But stepping back another moment after Eve's called out to me, let me explain something else. In case you're still wondering who "A.J." is; it's me. She's called me that since way-back-when. I think it all began when we finally settled on our full names for each other. And, of course, she was most instrumental in their final selection.

The process of selecting them began one day when she said: "Adam, you've got to have a middle and last name."

"Why?" I asked. "You're the only one here. We're absolutely alone on this entire world. Who would you confuse me with? I sure can't get lost in a crowd."

"I know. I know," she replied, somewhat impatiently. "But that most likely won't always be the case. You just never know. And we can't be too prepared when it does happen."

"Yeah, I guess you're right," I acknowledged. "We just appeared. What's to say we won't run into a large herd of folks like us once we exit this here Garden? So what do you have in mind?"

"Well," she began, "I think 'James' should be your middle name. 'Adam James' has a nice, southern-sounding twang to it. And then for your last name, which I suppose should be mine as well, given that we related, in a rib-sharing sort of way, I thought of a real unusual sounding name."

Growing more excited by the moment, I gleefully asked, "What's that?!"

"Smith," she replied. Your full name should be 'Adam James Smith'"

"That sounds great!" I shouted. "By golly, Eve, you're a genius for sure. And coming up with such great names just proves it!

But, of course, little did we realize "Smith" was to become the most common name in the English-spoken language. In addition, I remember proudly thinking that it probably would be in common usage within other languages as well, once they were able to advance beyond their rudimentary beginnings. For example, I was to later learn that in the dominant Asian language, spoken by our then-neighbors to the east of Eden, they initially chose surnames that sounded more like the warm-up notes for an operatic singer: "DO, RA, ME, FA, SO, LA, TE and DO". What kind of imagination did it take to come up with names that sound like syllables? "Smith" had some body to it. It was a grand name.

And I was very proud Eve gave it to us, and I would eagerly answer to it thereafter.

However, then it came my turn to help give Eve her full name, some of which she of course already had adopted… the "Smith" portion. But I wanted to fill-out her first name, making it more formal for special occasions, like at the dedication of buildings, launching ships at sea and unveiling monuments. So I thought long and hard about that before I eventually made my suggestion.

And finally, I yelled out, "I've got it! I know what you're full name should be: 'Even-Steven Smith'. I lengthened your first name just a little, added a nice matching middle name, and completed it with our surname. What do you think?"

"Gad!" she cried out. "Why couldn't you have chosen something like'Evelyn', 'Evangeline'or 'Eventide'? And 'Steven'… that's not a woman's name; at least not yet it isn't!"

"Well," now somewhat dejected at my gallant attempt, I ventured, "What would you suggest?"

"We are going to leave my first name as it is: 'Eve'. I like the tonal quality about it. It seems to resonate with meaning that implies 'the beginning' or 'the first', and it has a singular beauty surrounding it as well. Just call me 'Eve', and I'll be very pleased with that."

"Right!" I agreed, knowing full-well even then in those earliest of days together that I had better do so. Already, I sensed that there were only certain things amongst womenfolk that someone like me could forcefully argue for. As for instance, they might be topics concerning the weather, fixing car engines, who's the best wingback for the local footie team or who makes the best beer. It definitely is not arguing for what a woman's name should be; 'Eve Smith' it was.

So, getting back to Eve calling out to me on that first, early morning, after we just arrived in New York City's Central Park, I stretched, yawned and answered, "Over here, love; I'm resting up against this lovely Sugar Maple tree. And I'm pleased you've had such a nice nap. You definitely needed it. I think both of us are able to relax a little more right now, knowing that this is our last survey… ever. We are done after this one!"

"I know," she replied. "And I'm sure you're probably the same, but I'm completely played out. I don't want to even think back how long we've been doing all this appearing, birthing and then reappearing for these surveys. It has to end. While it's true neither of us appear to others like we're much past distinguished, middle age; inside we must be almost petrified by now."

"Yeah," I agreed. "I feel truly 'stoned'… as in marbleized. All anyone needs to do is prop me up on a pedestal somewhere, and I'd probably look like one of those city-square statues."

"But despite our feeling so exhausted and my momentary confusion," Eve pressed, "I must ask you, 'where exactly are we now?' And would you just look at me?… and YOU! We've got to get something to wear that is more appropriate than these imitation bear-skin overcoats and knee-high, lace-up climbing boots that we wore on our last assignment before coming here. While it was still frigid on that world; it obviously feels like the middle of summer here. And it's still early in the morning! What is it going to be like this afternoon? We've got to get more appropriate clothing, A.J.!"

"Hold on a minute," I exclaimed. "Let me begin by answering your first question. By my rough calculation, we are presently located in Central Park, the closest thing in this metropolis to Eden that I was able to find to make you feel somewhat more at home, seeing how this is to be our very last stop. We can make our usual inspections and do our customary interviews at eight to ten different locations around this island of Manhattan, and then we'll be done... for good. I hoped to make this last world's survey as easy as possible for us.

"But, honestly, as I look around me, all I see are tall buildings. It's like we're in a prison compound of some sort. Rather than stone walls, the city instead has erected buildings to keep the park's greenery inside, like they were afraid it might escape and leave them without any reminder of what living plants and standing water smelled or looked like. This park is like a world unto itself, and the metropolis surges around it. In fact, I bet once we get a little further into the day, this place will fill up with people. Already, I'm beginning to see more people riding bicycles and jogging along special pathways.

"And, you're right, I agree about our clothes. I gave you my coat to lie on; otherwise I'd be sweltering too. So, if it's ok with you, I'll head into the city, find a clothing store and get us something more in season to wear while we're here. How does that sound?"

"You bet. Get me something cool, light and comfortable. And get us something to eat. I'm famished."

"Consider it done, my sweet. I'll be off and plan on returning within the hour with food and clothes for both of us."

Without paying much attention to any of my surroundings, at least only enough to allow me to find Eve again, hidden as she was in a small grove of trees, off one of the pathways and about ten yards from a small arched, stone bridge, I took off and soon found both a discount clothing store and within the same block a take-out diner. And as promised, within an hour I was back, having already changed into my newly purchased clothes in the store. I just left the clothes I had been wearing with the clerk; with instructions to give them to someone she thought might need them. She asked me if I had just come from a mountain climbing expedition. I simply smiled and said in my best broken English that it had been more a surveying party than an expeditionary one. I doubt it satisfied her curiosity, but to go into more detail would have compromised our mission. She would know EVERYTHING soon enough.

Completely out of breath, due to my wanting to get back to Eve as quickly as possible, I was literally running by the time I reached the little bridge, next to where she was hidden. And as I ducked into the bushes and trees sheltering her, I held out both arms and exclaimed, "TA-DAA! I return with food and clothing for the Madam!"

"Oh, Adam James, what have you done?" Eve moaned. Look at you! You're dressed like some aged surfer, completely lost on the beach, somewhere in Hawaii. You're wearing a half-buttoned, flower-covered shirt with baggy shorts to match; open-toed sandals, and an over-sized straw hat. And your sun-glasses make you look like a hoot-owl on steroids. I hesitate to ask what you got for me."

Only minimally deterred by her initial reaction, because by now I was well aware that was so often the case with most things I did, I happily replied, "Well, for you, my pet, I got a lovely one-piece outfit. The store clerk said they were all the rage right now."

"Hold it up and let me look at it," Eve requested, with resignation building quickly in her voice. "My heavens, it's only the length of a sun dress, ending well-above my knees. It's a coolot! And it, too, has a print design with huge, flowering white and yellow daisies! Is there anything subtle about you, A.J.!! And look, you got me sandals as well!! I guess I should feel lucky you didn't get me a bathing suit instead. Oh, Adam, you're precious. But you couldn't dress an Eskimo for a driving snow storm. You'd have him wearing sun-tan lotion and boxer shorts. But I love you anyway. And I will wear what you've so lovingly brought me. Here, let me put it on, and then let's eat. I'm starving, and I can only guess how hungry you must be."

It was only after our breakfast that I shared with Eve what had been said to me when I went shopping for our clothes earlier that day. The worrisome conversation with her went something like this:

"Evie."

"Yes, A.J."

"Something was said by the clerk in the clothing store where I bought our clothes today."

"Oh. That's nice. Did she compliment you on how sporting you looked once you changed clothes?"

"No, nothing like that. It happened when I was about to leave the store and had just opened the door to exit. She called out to me saying, 'Let me be the first to welcome you, stranger, TO THE BIG APPLE!!!'"

"And..."

"Come on, Eve. That's how all our planetary and Universal roaming got started; from me taking that itty-bitty bite out of that teensy-weensy APPLE!!! Now, for heaven's sake, we're marooned INSIDE someplace called THE BIG APPLE. It's like we've come full circle, that The Creator is still testing us. It's like we're being reminded of something in our past, something that is still so humbling. It's like before we make this final survey and give our very last summation to the entire world that we are being reminded, 'we, too, once faulted and failed; that we're not perfect, and that it is not our place to sit in judgment on this or any other world'.

"Honestly, it's got me spooked. Us… sitting here eating breakfast inside THE BIG APPLE… I just don't know. It's got me spooked."

"Hmmm… I see your point. It does seem too coincidental. Our lives do appear to be coming full circle. And lest we forget, we have been put on notice to observe and make our recommendations carefully and compassionately. We've not been sent on this journey through the infiniteness of time and space to judge whoever we meet and whatever we find. We're here to help hold up a giant, world-size mirror for everyone to see themselves as someone coming from outside Earth would and to hold out a promise of what can and should be seen, if that image has become distorted and misshapen.

"We didn't pick these particular places we come to for these surveys. And you being welcomed with those words this morning is a way of emphasizing that point. It's clear, dear heart, that we must make absolutely sure what we are about to do and how we go about doing it. Let me think a minute or two, while I change into these new clothes that you bought me. Maybe you can clean up around the area while I'm doing that. It's time to get ready for our last and possibly our most important survey and final announcement.

THE INSPECTION BEGINS

THREE: HOW TO PROCEED

And sure enough, it wasn't more than fifteen minutes later that Eve called me over to where she had been jotting down some notes and asked me to sit down. In that short amount of time she had organized how we were to approach this final, upcoming challenge of our incredibly long lifetime.

"I've decided that we should make our usual inspections and interviews in at least ten different locations around this island," she began. "From the promptings I'm being given by The Creator, this city must represent a microcosm of human interaction and progress, or the lack thereof, for this entire world. In fact, this metropolis we're about to examine sufficiently represents all of humanity's attempts to establish peace and harmony within itself. And apparently it also will serve as an eventual indicator for how all intelligent life will behave and progress in the other worlds we've surveyed up until now. Because this was our first world to populate, it has the potential to tell us how other younger worlds will evolve. From what I understand, that is why we have ended up here for our very last accreditation visit and why it is such a pivotal survey."

"That seems too daunting a task for me," I replied. "It's more than my simple brain can comprehend. I'm getting progressively more confused. Besides, how are we supposed to accomplish all that and still be fair and thorough at the same time?"

"Good question. And to insure that we are, we'll each spend one day at one or more different locations for the next five days. Come Saturday, we will have to review what we've seen and heard and maybe try to get some rest. Then on Sunday we will announce our findings to everyone. Today's inspections could most likely be the shortest, due to our getting a later start. Usually, we should be on station by 6 a.m., and work until at least 6 p.m., if not beyond, depending on our assignment. Staying longer might help you get a better idea of both the people and their circumstances. In that way, we should meet and interview a good cross-section of people and get their reactions to and compliance with all the standards and criteria we have used in the past. However, for this last inspection, I have expanded our list of standards somewhat. We can go over them momentarily.

"We will start out each morning from our present location, here in the woods adjacent the Conservatory Garden Pavilion at East 105th Street and 5th Avenue. For today, I'll catch the Number 1 bus on 5th Avenue, which should take me to 42nd street, where the New York City Public Library is located. And after spending a good portion of the day there, tomorrow I'll either walk to or catch the Number 4 bus to investigate the large museums in this immediate area. Knowing you, you'll probably want to just walk the twenty blocks up to 125th Street to begin your first day's survey of Harlem.

"But, before we get started this morning, I have to spend some time with you going over our list of standards. I will give you a clip board with them outlined, so you can initially make notes as to how you find the people and the conditions in each location. As in previous surveys, you'll probably get so you don't need to use it and can just make mental notes to record from later when we come back here each evening. But before the morning gets away from us, let me quickly go over this list:

"1. Behaving:

<u>Age</u>: <u>Common Conditions/Landmarks Possible</u>:

0-5 years: Inquisitive, rapid developmental stage, bonding with parents, brimming with love and trust, full of wonder at the world around them.

6-11 years: Exploratory, gradual separation from earlier attachments, forming opinions and absorbing patterns exhibited/reinforced by family/caregivers.

12-19 years: Independence progresses, with a particularly unique individual behavior pattern emerging. Upon occasion, a possessiveness or selfishness develops as an individual tries to cope with threats, changes, demands and challenges to surmount. Fixed patterns of behavior for good or ill are forming.

20-29 years: These are significant years; a sense of self emerges with goals, dreams and aspirations forming and being worked toward: for good or ill. Heroic-type behavior becomes evident.

30-49 years: Modification of behaviors and aspirations will be initiated. The ultimate success or failure of someone is often determined during this period. Mistakes made before and during this time must be addressed. The very substance of an individual is at stake during this period.

50-64 years: A person's more steady-state, productive years, unless there has been a behavioral paralysis or calamity and the individual is stuck in an earlier phase. By now it is clear how well the years of one's personal behavior was self-monitored and managed. Personal success or failure is evident by this time.

65-on years: A steady or very rapid decline in health and a dependency first experienced in early childhood. The awareness of having been truly loved and of knowing how to return that love will allow graceful entry into, passage throughout and graduation from this final period in one's life.

"2. Adapting:

0-5 years: This is a wondrous time of continuous adapting to one's environment and to family and strangers. It's a non-stop process: globally within the individual.

6-11 years: The process continues at a

steady pace, but now becoming more specialized: learning skills, social interactions outside the immediate family unit.

12-19 years: Earliest beginnings of resistance to adaptation. Some fixed behaviors are being established, especially social, ethnic and religious. A tendency to be less open to change can be developing.

20-29 years: This period begins to separate the open-minded from the closed. This is a pivotal time in the process of adaptation. Fear of change and of different points of view can become threatening or the individual will acknowledge that change is to be expected in all aspects of life.

30-49 years: A pattern is now well established as to whether change is a threat or analyzed and adapted, if found beneficial. Maturity becomes the hallmark of this period.

50-64 years: The benefit of coping with a lifetime of change is exhibited during this time, or most likely, the individual has fallen by the way or is now very ill.

65-on years: Change becomes less welcome and the agility and ability to cope or adapt to it less and less likely.

"3. Caretaking:

0-5 years: Not applicable. This is essentially the time of total care. Bonding to family will eventually lead to wanting to care for others, if not interrupted by abuse or abandonment.

6-11 years: Minimal to noticeable sense of obligation to help with the care of those around the individual now seen. Rare examples of heroic acts and obvious caretaking of siblings and/or pets will become evident in some.

12-19 years: A sincere and often a lifelong sense that the common good of society is important, but adolescent selfishness and self-preoccupation can overwhelm all altruistic beginnings. Volunteering and a commitment to serve others can begin now.

20-29 years: The cross-roads in caretaking. Radicalization of personality, as a result of environmental and childhood experiences and educational opportunities or the lack thereof, will now be obvious. This small minority make life a living hell for far too many.

30-49 years: Altruism is now ingrained and/or rejected. Manipulation, disappointments, divorce, poverty or death of loved ones take their toll or they can motivate and inspire.

50-64 years: This is often the period of the greatest and most sustained contribution.

65-on years: Progressively more needed for themselves rather than of others.

"4. Sharing:

0-5 years: Earliest beginnings of this activity seen. Significant factor is the presence or absence of other siblings or contemporaries at this age. Likewise, teaching and example by family and elders is important.

6-11 years: Family influence dominates: welcoming strangers, mother/father interactions, cultural restraints and biases. The appearance of prejudices is now in its formative stages.

12-19 years: Individual can become isolated within a small party: immediate family members; a gang, cell, club. Or the individual can begin to reach out more readily to others, including strangers.

20-29 years: Another critical stage: the individual can become radicalized or resistant to helping anyone beyond a select group. Selfish and destructive patterns become uncompromising.

30-49 years: Healthy patterns established with family, neighbors, work site, religious affiliation and community.

50-64 years: A definite imprint exists by now: either sharing is natural or it isn't.

65-on years: Happiness and a sense of well being predicated on capacity to share easily.

"5. Learning:

0-5 years: Probably the highest level of this activity in an individual's life. A process of skill acquisition through imitation dominates; rather than interactive learning with discourse, debate and compromise, which all come later. Impediments to this stage are secondary to constitutional factors, e.g. hereditary, birth injury or environmental conditions.

6-11 years: Now begins to form word associations, analysis skills and recognize relationships. Writing composition, playing musical instruments and singing begun in earnest.

12-19 years: Definite traits and skills or lack thereof are emerging. Successful learning processes or learning difficulties are well exposed by now, as demonstrated by students' behavior. Acquisition of new skills and comprehension of material is not accomplished with learning by rote. Learning has to incorporate discussion, debate and compromise.

20-29 years: More in-depth, complicated, critical and causal learning, including becoming aware of how to learn and avoiding that which results in often self-destructive behaviors, habits and consequences.

30-49 years: Height of the learning curve reached and an established pattern of openness to new ideas or methodology and a mature questioning of all dogma. Progressive development of an individual's sense of humor is seen, which is one of the hardest of learned traits.

50-64years: Steady-state learning seen, along with the ability to adapt to new situations or accepting limitations and realizing missteps taken in the past. Self-deprecating humor or the ability to see oneself as a ready source of comedy is a key indication of someone now being a learned individual.

65-on years: Never ceases, if mental faculties will allow. Recall less facile, requiring the use of props and perseverance.

"6. Remembering:

0-5 years: Critical stage in development: the ability to profit from what was previously learned, including such activities as nourishment, comfort, affection and acceptance.

6-11 years: Developing more acute

awareness of surroundings and can reproduce more complicated tasks.

12-19 years: Developing memories of intricate tasks and events. Able to interconnect cause and effect, establish logical relationships, allowing one to act responsibly.

20-29 years: Peak time of memory development and recall.

30-49 years: Can begin to develop excuses for not following accepted social mores, tenets, laws, principles and standards.

50-64 years: Needing more cues to remember. Less agile with the need to "replace" some memories or "make room" for new ones.

65-on years: Less and less able to recall or remember with ease.

"7. Avoiding or Profiting from Mistakes:

0-5 years: Pivot time for trial and error.

6-11 years: Still needs constant reinforcement to avoid mistakes or errors and to apologize when appropriate.

12-19 years: Still making mistakes but self-correcting more frequently. Excuses are still accepted when mistakes occur.

20-29 years: Tolerance for excuses less and less. The timeframe when responsibility for self determines an individual's progress in other pursuits. Rationalization for causing harm to self and others can become fixed. This is a time when the crossroads of achieving full maturity reached.

30-49 years: Ability to confess, admit but not repeat mistakes is essential at this stage.

50-64 years: Mistakes by omission or commission are now possibly forgivable but not necessarily forgettable. Taking care with one's daily life is essential.

65-on years: The time when meeting this standard is obvious and ingrained.

"8. Exploring and Inventing:

0-5 years: Every waking moment dedicated to exploration. Inventiveness is seen by constantly assembling and rearranging objects, challenging oneself with more complex activities of daily living.

6-11 years: Now moving beyond bodily wants and needs into forays involving social interaction; most tentative and filled with embarrassment. Inventiveness manifested by some creativity now evident.

12-19 years: Now trying to balance between poor self-esteem and bullying arrogance through exploration of social contacts with contemporaries, family and the world at large. Creativity showing promise, e.g. music, the arts.

20-29 years: Exploration beyond self begins in earnest: asking "Why?" and "How?" for all that's around him or her. Now can clearly identify inventiveness and creativity: for good or ill.

30-49 years: The height of discovery, questioning, probing for answers to questions about this life and beyond. The most active time for inventiveness: simplicity of design merges with complexity of achieving it.

50-64 years: Ability to explore is beginning to face limitations in physical and mental capabilities. Overall, inventiveness is declining, but some late bloomers or stalwarts continue to press on.

65-on years: Exploration not a common activity, unless an inquisitive and restless mind still drives the individual. Only rarely does unparalleled excellence appear with inventiveness into this period.

"9. Governing:

0-5 years: Not applicable.

6-11 years: Minimal opportunity to regulate or control anything other than oneself. Influence over others minimal to none.

12-19 years: Formative beginnings of leadership, sense of fair play and acknowledgement of need for community's well being over self occur.

20-29 years: Awareness and zeal for radical alternatives to governing become solidified and acted on. Alternatively, others are becoming disciples of law, order and governance through studies, volunteering and professional occupations.

30-49 years: Careers involving the governing process become established. Every society's best and brightest choose public service at some point.

50-64 years: Productive years, if not sidelined by unrealistic goals or wayward behavior. The executive, legislative and legal centers are filled with these individuals. By now their true motivation of being there is evident and the results of that choice are clear. Their decisions are often the best of difficult or painful choices.

65-on years: For the most part, it is now time to pass the governing torch on to the next generation. But there is much to say for tradition, precedent and history. The character of a community, state or nation is a balance between new ideas and established and proven habits. Neither can dominate the governing process.

"10. Loving:

0-5 years: Dependence steadily merges into trust and love within the family unit.

6-11 years: Signs of independence and closer associations with non- family members intensifies.

12-19 years: Sharing, trust, openness become clearly evident with non-family members. Friendships become deeper, longer lasting.

20-29 years: Family relationships become more complex, even if more distant. Long-term commitments to someone outside family become more likely now.

30-49 years: Mature, honest love of another most likely taking place or at least this quest is in full gear. Only time will tell if each individual learns how to love and is worthy of selfless love: both the true test of an individual's maturity and soul.

50-64 years: Wondrous times or beginning of loneliness and isolation.

65-on years: Ability to give comfort, have compassion and experience serenity self-evident if this standard has been met during an individual's lifetime."

Once Eve had finished explaining this revised outline to me, I sighed deeply and replied, "You've really expanded this list. How am I supposed to remember and measure all these standards and criteria everywhere I go?"

"You're not," she answered. "I've decided we are to concentrate on only one standard for each of the ten locations. As an example, when you go to Harlem today, you are to focus entirely on the Behaving Standard. At the same time, I will be analyzing how humanity has met and is meeting the Learning Standard while at the New York City Public Library, in various public venues, at a local University and in the public and private schools, grades one through twelve."

"Ok", I acknowledged, "That seems straightforward enough. But how am I supposed to do any scoring for what I surveyed? Forgive me, but I'm getting more confused by the minute with your updated version of these standards. It seems like the most difficult and complex accreditation has been saved for the last one. And I'm afraid I will foul it all up."

"Well, I have to admit," Eve began, "the scoring is fairly different from what we've done in the past. Basically, it is based on 70 being the highest score that can be achieved for any one standard. On the other hand, if the standard achieved only the lowest score, its score would be a 10. So, in summation, the points for each age-related category values are: 10 points for 0 to 5 years; 20 points for 6 to 11 years; 30 points for 12 to

19 years; 40 points for 20 to 29 years, 50 points for 30 to 49 years; 60 points for 50 to 64 years and 70 points for 65 years on.

"So, as an example, say you eventually decided that your survey of humanity, as represented by people you met today in Harlem, deserved a Behaving Standard score of 40 points. This would indicate that a collective maturity of a 20 to 29 year old individual has been achieved. And say I found in my inspection today that humanity has earned a Learning Standard score of 30 points. In this case it would be equivalent to a 12 to 19 year old individual. Taken together, that would mean the total score for today for all of humanity would be 70. And we would have eight more standards to survey to get the final total.

"Probably I should remind you, as we have had to do amongst ourselves repeatedly during and after all our previous surveys, a higher final score does not indicate that a society or world is approaching senility or full-fledged geriatric status in some way, if it reaches a higher plateau. The higher the final score only indicates the more reconciled, mature and at peace that particular world has become.

"And of course, once our ten surveys are completed, we both will have to prepare a statement to go along with the announcement of our findings and whether we can grant renewed accreditation to this world, the one we have so longed to come back and investigate.

"All we can do is hope that over the

countless years that we've been away, the people of this magnificent world have gained a full appreciation of its beauty and uniqueness and an accompanying maturity to live each day peacefully and to govern wisely. They must have done so, if they are to continue occupying it."

MONDAY

FOUR: HAREM… hmm, HARLEM

I have to tell you that hearing all of Eve's explanation and instructions, plus being given a clip board and some sheets of paper to write any comments on before I made my decision as to how I would assess humanity's compliance with this first standard, I was still pretty bewildered. Even having practiced doing this drill countless times before, it had not prepared me for the reality that this was our LAST TIME and the consequences it held for ALL THE PEOPLE on this most-special of all planets. On second thought, I was overwhelmed.

And it didn't help to realize again that in human years, each one of yours can't even remotely be compared to one of Eve's and mine. Just give that a little thought, will you? It wasn't enough that we had initiated the present inhabitant's journey on this precious world. Of course even saying that, I'm not forgetting about there being some MAJOR involvement by our All-Knowing and Ever-Loving Creator as well. But now, some gazillion years later, we had to determine if it was worth that initial effort of ours. In short, we were about to assess if you deserved continuing on your merry way or if you needed a drastic mid-course correction or maybe, heaven forbid, warranted a cancellation of your permit to "Continue Occupancy on These Premises".

And yes, it's true. We've had to issue a few rather bland warnings in the past. Things were simply about to get out of hand after we left some of those now-occupied worlds. I guess the folks began to think they could just do anything, without considering there might be consequences. Unfortunately for them, they were wrong. Eve and I had to turn on a giant, yellow caution light for all of them to see. And if they didn't understand what we sensed was happening, their situation certainly could have become direr. Luckily, just a few cautionary words were necessary. Each world quickly responded to our prodding. Happily, we've never had to issue a stern warning that immanent closure was at hand. And we can't imagine having to do anything even remotely like that with your world. It was, as I've noted repeatedly, and still is, our favorite. And we anticipate you will pass with flying colors.

Even with my feeling all this, I still had the awesome responsibility to uphold my end of this examination. I'm sure each of you has faced a similar kind of situation: one that at the time seemed far beyond your capability and pay grade, but you still had to proceed. So, with a heavy sigh, I gave Eve our customary, beginning-of-the-day-hug, smiled wanly at her and headed out of the woods towards Fifth Avenue, where I began walking north to my day's assignment.

Immediately upon stepping onto Fifth Avenue, I was surrounded by people; a few were walking briskly, most were running, and countless others were in or on vehicles of all shapes and sizes. Taken together, it seemed as if they were going in all directions at once. I've seen disturbed hornets, after their nests have been given a sudden jolt, scurry and scatter less frantically. It appeared to me like a decree or city ordnance had been issued, requiring that you had to move as fast as you could to get somewhere… anywhere, before someone else did. Certainly, seeing this prompted me to want to reach for my clipboard and make an initial comment about this remarkable behavior, but I wasn't sure where I was, other than somewhere about one hundred feet from where Eve and I first arrived. It seemed too early to start making notations. I knew my day's destination had to be further away than this. So I just made a mental note: 'So far, it appears that no one here knows how to walk slowly'.

Anyway, Eve had told me that I probably

needed to walk north some distance before I got to my assigned area for the day; but it was unclear to me how far "northward" I'd have to go before getting there. One thing was certain, I sure didn't look like anyone else, dressed as I was. But, somehow, I didn't feel so out of place. Sure, there were the usual number of folks who stopped and stared at me, but I'd always just nod my head and smile back at them as they did. Interestingly, that seemed to kind of disarm them; it was almost as if my smiling at them was more unnerving than the way I was dressed. And yet, overall, their staring and whispering didn't seem as frequent as Eve seemed to imply that it might be. So, by the time I reached 120th Street, I was feeling reasonably proud of myself and of my choice of clothing.

But about then, I sensed that there was another more serious matter at hand. I was lost. There were no signs that announced where Eve had told me to go. Or if there were, there were so many other signs telling you what to do, not to do, where to go, where not to go, what to buy, where to shop and yes, what to wear, that I got totally confused and knew that I was hopelessly lost. And I've learned that over the course of my lifetime, when I feel lost, I truly am.

Imagine yourself having to travel across the expanse of the Universe and well-beyond, and tell me that you'd have any real sense of direction. What's up? Or Down? What's it matter if you're supposed to go a few "blocks", miles, kilometers or light-years? After a while, you don't have any reference point. My internal compass and the capacity to know precisely my location, or even to remember the names of locations where I was instructed by Eve to go, become entangled within a mind that had by then lost all bearings. And whenever it reached a point of my being paralyzed, I would just stop and look bewildered in all directions. Eventually, if I was lucky, someone came to my rescue.

And coincidentally, given that my first assignment was to survey the Behavior Standard and the fact that I was now hopelessly lost, I had been given a golden opportunity to begin my day's work. I needed help. I was eager to see what might happen next.

To the credit of the people who lived in that area, wherever it was, and the same to the masses of people who lived on this world and were about to be painstakingly examined by Eve and I, within a matter of minutes three young men came up to me and asked, "Mister, you look really lost."

"Indeed I am," I replied, relieved that someone noticed so quickly.

"Where are you going?" the taller one of the group asked, edging up closer, while peering down at me.

You need to keep in mind that neither Eve nor I are very tall. Both she and I, "The Originals", as I frequently refer to us in her presence, are only about four feet tall. When we made our rather suddenly appearance to any world, we were always the First Ones anywhere. Consequently, any mention of our being height-challenged or possibly experiencing some size-discrimination was not an issue anywhere. Occasionally someone might have commented on the style of clothes I chose to wear, or initially the lack thereof, but no one ever commented on our stature.

So when I mention that this one fellow was looking down at me, I mean he was really looking down… straight down.

"Well," I said, in a manner and tone that I thought might impress him with the importance of my presence and mission, both of which I was forbidden to divulge, "I'm looking for harem."

Now, I wish you could have seen their expression when I said that. I could have been freely distributing one thousand dollar bills.

"A HAREM!!" they all three shouted simultaneously. "MAN!!! What kind of dude are you?!" the taller one burst out. "You're what we'd consider around here as being a bit short… no offense meant of course. But can you beat this; you want to find a HAREM! You've got to be THE MAN!"

Of course, I had no idea what or who "the man" was, but it did sound like someone that obviously impressed these fellows, so I didn't object or correct them. I was simply relieved that they might get me headed in the right direction… me finding my way.

Then the shorter of my three potential rescuers, but someone still a good foot or two taller than me, asked in a puzzled sort of way, "What in the world are you going to do when you find it?"

"Oh," I answered, "it's really quite straight forward; I'll evaluate the premises and the people occupying themselves there. I'm actually on a kind of mission."

"EVALUATE!!" came the stunned response, again from all three.

"What a unique and creative way to describe your so-called mission once you are inside such an assemblage. How many of these have you found or been to before?" the taller fellow asked.

"Probably thousands," I replied, as I watched them back away in total awe.

Trying to catch their collective breath, the taller fellow, whose name I later learned was Bob Davis, breathlessly asked, "How often do you actually do these inspections?"

"On average lately, once every week," I proudly answered.

After hearing this as a group, I thought their knees were going to buckle; and they would collapse on the sidewalk. Finally, collecting themselves, they cried out in unison, "YOU'RE DEFINITELY THE MAN! AND WELCOME TO HARLEM."

Of course, it was at this point that I became so relived at the direction this little conversation was going. I exclaimed that indeed it was Harlem that was my destination, but that never, for as long as they chaperoned me through that bustling area, did they believe that I wasn't actually still looking for a harem.

Later on, I learned that they secretly thought I was being polite and a gentleman, not wanting to be overly exhibitionist about my cosmic exploits. It wasn't until I relayed this encounter to Eve that she enlightened me as to my mistake. But inadvertently, it served to give me three, very fine guides, and ultimately, much more for my survey of that teeming part of Manhattan and elsewhere beyond its borders..

From that introduction, until I left Harlem late that night, these three intrepid scouts led me to all the areas I needed to see and to survey. Some areas were not on my list of "must go to", but one of them, the barber shop in particular, served my purposes well.

You see, I have ignored one aspect of my general appearance for a very long time. And Eve doesn't mention it any longer, because she has given up doing so. And I realize that it's another 'guy' thing. It involves my beard, the length of my hair and the fact that at the time we began this final survey, I had a great deal of both. Honestly, probably sheering most sheep wouldn't have yielded as much wool when you compared it to the amount of hair my barber cut off that same morning in Harlem.

"How much hair?" you might ask. Imagine, if you will, someone's beard and hair both hanging down past his waist. For me, it helped define who I was. Eve always said I must look like what Rip Van Winkle did after he woke up... whoever he was. She always amazed me with the names and references to people, places and things that I had never seen nor heard of before. In my defense, after she explained about ole Rip's circumstances, I countered that mine was a source of strength and had taken eons to grow. His only took twenty years, and he was asleep the entire time! In reply, Eve just shook her head at my endless rationalizations.

And frankly, after those few months when we first became partners, she has never seen me without a full mane and beard. Probably, if there are any analysts out there reading this account, they probably would suggest that I was really trying to hide from that shameful, Apple-eating business. But this being our very last survey, I knew it was time to make a change I needed to get a tailored haircut and trim, along with a smooth-faced shave. Eve would be so proud of me for doing so. And I couldn't wait to see her reaction once I did.

Immediately after our initially greeting each other, the shorter of my three escorts commented on the length of my hair and suggested that maybe I'd like to see a local barber. But he added that he wasn't intending to offend me or somehow interfere with my upcoming visit to a harem or to Harlem.

Given that I had just decided to do that sometime soon, I agreed to let my escorts take me to the nearest barber for a long overdue haircut and shave.

My entrance into a large barber shop around 125th Street was met with an audible gasp. Inside, there were ten barber chairs, all of which were occupied. The first impression I had was of the stunning mixture of odors and fragrances. It was like everything I had ever smelled, from those first, long-ago years in Eden until that moment, came wafting by me. Aged wooden cabinets; decades of cigar, pipe and cigarette smoke, each of which was now strictly forbidden by city ordinance signs posted everywhere; and a blend of colognes, perfumes, hair rinses, powders and working men's sweat greeted me as I walked inside. The mixture was welcoming. It said that the past was honored in this place; that stories and tales, some true, many exaggerated, would be shared and equally listened to and honored.

I thought to myself about how Eve described the advent of modern day beauty salons, where an upscale, rushed and modern day clientele breezed in and out, ever concerned about their immediate looks and upcoming appointments. Inside this refuge, there was an insistence that you stay and share. No conversation or topic was off-limits; no urgency to meet some impossible deadline existed; no occupation or lack thereof was recognized or honored more than another. It was a small enclave of what a democratic and free exchange of ideas was about. And I immediately felt at home once I stepped inside.

Once we got inside, Robert, as he preferred to be called, went over and whispered something to one of the barbers. Once that was done, he then came back and had all of us take a seat in some of the twenty or so chairs, the few of which were still empty. And from then on our conversations were animated and, surprisingly, very helpful for me, given my assignment to explore the behaviors within this neighborhood. But before I could get too comfortable, there was a little flourish of activity followed by Robert nudging me and pointing to one of the barber chairs that was now empty. It was my turn. A murmur arose immediately as I stood and ambled over, my hair swishing back and forth now that I had removed my hat, under which a portion of my hair was tucked. Having become immune to Eve's comments about my long locks of hair and flowing beard, I assumed it was my newly acquired clothes that was causing the elevated tone in conversation. But I was wrong.

"How long did it take you to grow all that hair?" the barber asked, spinning the chair around so I faced the wall-to-wall mirror in front of the rows of chairs. It was a ritual that l noticed was repeated for each new customer.

"I couldn't really say," I replied. "My hair grows very slowly, but I'd have to guess something well over three to four hundred years."

That answer immediately quietened those cutting hair, those having it cut and those waiting their turn... as well as my three companions. "You're joking, of course," came the response behind me.

Thinking I may be getting over my head by that innocent and honest answer, I amended it with, "well, maybe not quite that long." And that was met with a round of laughter throughout the shop.

"So how much do you want me to cut, today?" came the next question.

And that was harder still to answer. After a rather lengthy pause, I finally said, "Just leave some bristle on top and shave my face clean!" I had never had my beard completely shaved off nor had I ever had my hair cut so short. It all sounded exciting, and I could just imagine how pleased Eve would be when she saw me.

"Do you have any idea how much all that hair is going to weigh once I cut it off?" the rather stunned barber asked.

"I couldn't guess for the life of me," I answered. "But why don't we have a bet to see who can guess the closest to the exact amount. Do you have a scale in here?"

"Yes, indeed, we do, and I think that is a great idea. Hey, fellows, this gentleman here is suggesting that each of us guess how much all his hair is going to weigh once it is cut off."

That was met with a round of approving nods and chuckles; and the betting process began immediately, with one of my three companions collecting the wagers. Before he began the removal process, the barber had me stand down and go over to the floor scales and weigh myself. While I stood on it, three separate folks read my weight for confirmation. It was 158 pounds. Even for a small fellow, I have to admit, in recent eons I've been getting a little rotund. After all, I don't get the exercise I once did just doing these surveys, and then there was all that hair.

Finally, to get a better cutting angle, the barber put a booster chair on the seat of his chair; something they apparently used for children. It made me feel a little awkward, but no one in the shop commented. I took that gesture as a good omen for their upcoming survey score. They were all polite and courteous.

Then the hair cutting and shaving began. All the while the shop was filled with conversations centered more and more on me. And just before my getting shaved, someone asked how old I actually was, and did I have any family in the area or any children. None of my answers to those questions was going to sooth their uneasiness with my answer about how long my hair had been growing. But my pledge, ever-after that incident in The Garden with that blasted Apple, was to be forthright and honest. So I told them that I was approximately 550,000 years old using their calendar, that we had three children while living here before and approximately 16 billion great, great, great, etc. children living everywhere else. I concluded by telling them that my name was Adam James Smith and my wife's was Eve Smith.

All that information slowed down the pace of conversation considerably for a while, with no one bothering to counter me. I think they were probably concerned that I might become violent if they did. So, their conversations reverted to business, politics, sports, wives, girlfriends, weather and life in general. It was a rich conversational atmosphere, and I shut my eyes and just let the barber cut and shave to his heart's desire. My guess was that doing so was like him competing in the Tour de France of barbering, because when they weighed me after all this was done, I had lost twenty-two pounds! And I looked almost like a kid. The beard had hidden the fact that I appeared almost ageless. I always commented to Eve that she did, but this was the first time I saw myself in a mirror and without all the facial hair. I was excited about having her see me for the first time later that day.

Eventually, it was necessary for me to leave the shop, and there was quite a send-off when I walked out. My guess was that my being there would not soon be forgotten. But now it was time to pick up the pace of my Harlem survey. But at no time did my three guides leave me. If anything, they almost seemed like my guardians.

For the next three hours there was an onslaught of visits, interviews and impressions. They entailed me observing Harlem's residents' behaviors throughout a ten-to-fifteen square block area. Jamal, the shortest of my three companions, but certainly not to the degree that I am, or "J.L." as everyone else called him, provided the transportation. Or to be more accurate, his father did. His father owned his own taxi cab service, which specialized in providing service only in Harlem and the immediate neighborhoods surrounding it

J.L. informed me that he would "run a tab" for the day. However, he added, given all that I explained to them I intended to do, his father might just donate the gas and time. Privately, I wagered to myself that it also had something to do with my initial inquiry about where I might find a "harem".

Were they in for a MAJOR disappointment. My story, in that regard, is about as exciting as a tuna casserole. I don't have the capacity to fantasize, nor even the desire to do so. Eve has always been the gal for me. She keeps me centered and focused. The Creator knew what was good for me when Eve was brought into my life. Forget about the Apple Business. She's the brains and the motivation in our union. Me? I just seem to supply the daily diversions and unexpected happenings to our marriage. But none of them are on purpose or by design. Odd things just seem to happen around or to me. It's like having a hovering cloud of mistakes, mishaps and misfortunes that accompanies me wherever I go. I've become used to it by now. The "harem" episode is a prime example of what I'm referring to. So, I just let the three escorts think or imagine what they wanted. I have a hard enough time keeping my own thoughts in some kind of order.

Meanwhile, in that next, three-hour timeframe, during which my escorts ate a late lunch with J. L.'s father, I managed to meet with a group of business leaders in what they called "The Chamber of Commerce" office. It was in a modestly appointed office on 125th Street. This meeting was followed by two incidents that occurred within this same period of time, and each deserves some extra comment. They were a "pickup" basketball game and a street-corner/alleyway conversation. But despite what must seem like erratic occurrences and delays to any outsider reading this report, my surveys always seemed to proceed in an odd, orderly fashion. Let me explain.

The basketball game happened almost spontaneously. It seemed to develop as a kind of diversion; something to release a buildup of tension: mine as well as my cohorts. I later wished I had known about playing basketball eons ago. I loved playing it for about thirty minutes that afternoon. If I had known of its existence, quite likely that Eden Event might never have happened. I could have just dribbled the ball a while, shot a few hoops, maybe had a pick-up game with Eve and never thought once about wanting to snack on that Apple.

Hindsight... I have that in remarkable abundance. What I've always lacked is foresight. If I only had a little more of that, my litany of misadventures, including the one with that blasted Apple, would be fewer; and I'd be less of a headache to Eve. Bless her heart. I'm so blessed that someone understands and cares about me. I'd be lost without her.

But, I digress again. However, before I get too far into this sporting adventure, it might be helpful to set the stage how, where and who took part. After I left the Chamber of Commerce meeting, it was Alexander, or 'Axe', as he was called by his associates, who suggested that I looked tense and might enjoy seeing some "hoops" being played. Feeling a little disoriented and rather extended emotionally, despite not having the slightest idea about what he was referring to, I agreed. In retrospect, I probably thought 'hoops' were some animals at the local zoo. And my connection with animal and bird life had always been keen and relaxing. So, I said "sure".

That was all he needed to hear. The cab driver and my three companions let out a spirited yell, and we sped off some blocks away from my meeting and from where they had had an early lunch. Rounding a corner in a very densely packed area of tall apartment buildings that my escorts called the "projects", there was a cleared area where many people of all ages were playing. It was busy with activity. And off to one side there was a concrete pad with sturdy, metal uprights centered at each end. Near the top of each upright, there was secured a large board, with a metal ring attached to it and white netting hanging down from it. The concrete slab was marked off with some white lines. And running up and down this same area were about a dozen fellows throwing and bouncing a fairly large, round ball.

When the taxi stopped to park nearby, I was told by my excited comrades to hurry over to that same area. As soon as they exited the cab, they began yelling at the people running back and forth on the court. Almost immediately, everyone stopped and looked squarely at me.

Now, up to this point, I have avoided

purposely saying anything about the appearance of anyone who I've met or spent time with while in Harlem. I'm not charged to identify colors, shapes, sizes or types of people I meet and speak with while doing these surveys. For this particular assessment, I am simply to note their behavior patterns, no matter who displays them or what they are. Any other details are peripheral and inconsequential to an assignment.

But to contrast what took place in the next few minutes, to you the reader of this report, I need to tell you that without question I was by far the lightest skinned and, by any measurement, the shortest person on that playground. That had no effect on me. However, I could see that apparently their seeing my Hawaiian-style outfit caused everyone else to stop and stare straight at me. And once my associates and I walked close enough to the other players, my escorts blended completely into the mix of the other players. Looking straight up at their faces, peering down at me, I felt and no doubt looked like one of the rather odd characters in Snow White's ensemble. I was, without a doubt, a living and breathing White Dwarf, particularly when I looked up and around and then smiled broadly at them like I had just won the New York State Lottery.

It was J.L. who broke the stunned silence, announcing that my name was "A.J.". Saying that alone seemed to please the crowd, because they began to pat me gently on top of my head. Then Axe announced loudly that we'd come to play some ball, and asked if we could join in. There followed a spirited response of acceptance and some rearranging of who was on the two opposing teams. After that was done, J. L. turned and asked me if I'd like to play as well.

Never one to miss an opportunity to experience something new, I readily agreed. And he selected me for his team, while Robert took the leadership role of the other. And it was clear to me right away that Robert's team was much taller and probably quicker. J.L. would need help, if his team would have any chance to win this match up.

The game started easy enough with the fellows gracefully running back and forth, bouncing the ball around them as they ran. I noticed how easily they shifted it behind them, through their legs or around someone else and then jumped up and tossed it inside the metal hoop. Whenever that occurred, the one side would yell something to each other and then everyone would run to the other netted ring and someone else would try to throw the ball inside it. The game was absolutely fascinating. And after about five minutes of my running back and forth, I felt like I'd like to try bouncing, jumping and doing some throwing.

Understand that at that point I was at least two to three feet shorter than anyone else on that slab. And of course, I was running in thongs. But none of that mattered to me. I wanted to try. Likewise, understand that I had just had my first real haircut and full-facial shave. I was feeling sleek and primed. So what if I was nearing my

550,000[th] birthday soon. It was time to play ball!

Nodding to J.L. to pass me the ball after Robert's team had scored again and was beginning to pounce us, he shrugged, probably thinking it wouldn't do any harm; we were losing anyway. So, he bounced it to me. And to the amazement of everyone in that housing and sports complex, this miniature-excuse for a bleached-out adult, dressed like he was about to grab a surf-board and "do the curl", began pounding that round ball, skirting around the opposing team's players, doing behind-the-back dribbles, then between the legs ones; and finally I crouched and leaped up over Robert, who was defending their netted ring, and DUNKED THE BALL!!

Probably, anyone who saw my performance that day would forever know that gravity didn't exert the same force on me that it did for everyone else on that basketball court. It seemed to have selective properties that day, and for me it didn't exist at all. After a brief stunned silence, there followed yelling, jumping around, pats on my head and an even greater sense amongst my associates that my use of the word "harem" was no slip of the tongue. Finally, once the excitement of my first possession of the ball calmed down, the game resumed; and our team eventually won!

If Eve and I had any other assignments to fulfill after this last one on Earth, I would have begged her for a basketball to take with us. Next to Eve, I fell immediately in love with that game. And I was notably impressed with the graceful behavior of all who witnessed or played with us that day.

Following that experience, I asked if the fellows would drive me to one of the more stressed areas of Harlem and let me get out of the cab and be on my own for a while. I needed to interview as many residents as I could while being alone and unaccompanied. Something told me doing so was the only way that I could evaluate certain behaviors and circumstances that I had been observing prior to then. And what follows next in this report is a description of my fourth encounter with residents living in Harlem.

Reluctantly, the taxi cab's occupants let me out in an area that was obviously much less cared for and its occupants much less successful in whatever they attempted to pursue. Per my instruction before stopping, they then drove off to visit one of Robert's relatives who live not too far from where I would be.

Upon climbing out onto the sidewalk, next to an almost unrecognizable telephone booth due to all the layers of paint depicting rage, revolt and resolve, I entered the most devastating area of this assignment. It was a world of hustle and crime; poor decision-making and failure; brain-washing and terror; uncontrolled emotions and death. This was a place, doubtlessly not unlike others the world over, where human behavior had become deceiving, self-serving and too often, self-destructive.

Everywhere I looked were signs of despair and unyielding, fixed patterns of poor behavior. It could be bought or sold. It could be anticipated or sudden and indiscriminate. It ranged all the way from passive resignation to minute-by-minute stalking terror. And I was immediately confronted with two examples of both extremes.

Once I walked a little further onto the stained and crumbling sidewalk, I looked up into the faces of two individuals obviously leery of who or, in my odd-looking case, what had purposefully entered their pitiful corner of this hell. Drawing on my experience, gained over the eons of needing to establish instantaneous rapport, which then allowed me to examine the results of countless self-aware, life forms' abilities to establish and flourish in free and orderly societies, I knew my success in conducting this particular survey and possibly my ultimate survival depended on my being absolutely direct, despite my outlandish appearance, mixed with a comical and unpredictable nature. In short, I had to be forthright and non-judgmental.

"Good afternoon," I began. "My name is Adam J. Smith, and I and my wife, Eve, have just arrived today in your city. She and I are involved in conducting a survey that will, we hope, eventually allow reaccreditation of your world, and as a good-faith token of my honesty and integrity, I offer you a sign. It is not magic nor a gesture of whimsy. It is real, and it is intended to serve as my introduction and pledge to you that I mean you no harm and will not compromise your very delicate hope that there possibly still may be any useful meaning to living."

And while these two forlorn people were staring down at me, still surprised enough at my appearance and size to have not yet decided what to say or do, I extended my right arm out fully to the side and waved my clinched fist in a large circle. Promptly and without a sound, there appeared before them a radiant, faceless form, dressed in flowing, white chiffon, partially suspended in mid-air. And before the two bystanders could speak or move, she spoke; her voice was soothing but richly textured with the tone of absolute authority.

"No harm is to come to you. And only the two of you can see me at this moment. Listen to what Adam has to say and answer his questions honestly. Do this, and avoid any further criminal behavior, and your lives will be touched with mercy and good fortune. Disobey this request, and you will experience a sudden and irreversible decline in anything and everything you attempt. And as a token of this pledge, I will touch each of you; and you will note a calming effect, which will persist for the rest of your lives, provided you heed my request."

And then the graceful figure, in a movement hardly visible to the naked eye, reached forward with some object and touched each individual on their forehead. And as quickly as that occurred, I dropped my arm, and she was gone.

"Pardon the theatrics, but my time is short; and I needed your fullest cooperation. You will note a new sensation of calm and peacefulness has replaced the ones of suspicion and distrust. And let me assure you, no one else has seen or heard anything but the three of us standing here. And it won't take me long to ask what I need to know."

For the next ten minutes I questioned the two, and their answers were obviously quite candid and helpful. When we completed our session, they asked how long Eve and I would be in town and what would happen with the information we were gathering. I quickly suggested that they should be seated in St. Patrick's Cathedral's mammoth sanctuary this coming Sunday at 4 p.m. and find out for themselves. Further, I noted that Eve and I will give a summation of our findings at that time, and if any deficiencies were found, suggest how some possible improvements can be made.

Hurriedly, after meeting with these two individuals, I walked up the street one block to where a small group of women were standing, some on the street's curb and some back away in a sheltered alleyway. They called out to me as I approached. But by the time I was facing them, I had pointed my arm again and my transforming archangel had altered their suspicion of why I was going to make contact with them; and in the process had immediately changed the direction of their lives henceforth. Our discussion lasted another informative, thirty minutes. Likewise, as with the just concluded meeting a block away, this one saddened me as well. It was painful, intermixed with growing sadness, for me to hear about the desperate circumstances of their daily lives. And before I departed, I requested my periodically appearing, gossamer-dressed associate speak with a certain male individual who drove up and yelled something profane and threatening at me while I was talking with these individuals. I doubt he heeded what he was advised to do, and undoubtedly within a matter of minutes his life and career objectives were about to take a sudden turn. It was no idle threat he was given. And as he drove away, I saw the vehicle he was driving suddenly swerve and come to a complete stop. His moment had arrived. And, following that, the women I had just spoken with were also given invitations to the upcoming Sunday announcement to be given by Eve and me.

Immediately thereafter, I waved at J.L's father's taxi, and it sped over to where I was standing. After climbing in and assuring them that I was doing fine, I asked that during the next four hours I needed to visit a walk-in health clinic, three homes, an elementary, middle and high school and end my day sometime around 7 p.m. at a church I noticed on the corner of 127th and Madison Avenue. My day in Harlem ended at 10 p.m.; after my meeting with a Bible study group and taking in a pot-luck, fellowship dinner at the church.

Everyone else I saw the rest of that day and evening was also given a personal invitation to the Sunday gathering at St. Patrick's. I was informed by the church's minister that this next Sunday was Easter Sunday. I thanked her but did not acknowledge that I was already aware of that fact. I assured her, and those gathered together for this evening's fellowship, that Eve's and my meeting would not infringe on anyone's previously scheduled, Easter morning's services   And to ensure that everyone I had seen or met that day was also invited, I asked my three helpful escorts for the day to please issue the same invitation to the individuals who I met at the barber shop and on the basketball court.

At their insistence, I was driven back to Central Park, to 105th Street and Fifth Avenue. As I was closing the cab's door, I thanked them profusely for their help and guidance throughout the day. And as I did, Axe asked me what time I was planning on leaving the next day, and where I was going. Surprised, I said around 6 a.m., and that I would be heading to various hospitals, nursing homes and possibly the prison on Rykers Island. And with that, I thanked them again and wished them well, thinking that I might see them once more on Sunday, when I could express my sincerest gratitude for their help that first day... one last time. However, as happened so often during my surveys, I misjudged the kindness of strangers. I was wrong.

FIVE: THE LEARNING STANDARD

I was beginning to worry about how late it was getting, when Adam suddenly burst through the undergrowth where we were camping. It was a relief to see him. Given his talent of getting into situations way over his head, I worried that I might have to rescue him… if he was delayed much longer. But he came bustling into our campsite all enthused and animated, as usual, about his day's investigations.

And then I saw him in the dim glow of the surrounding street lights.

"A.J.!! IS THAT YOU??!!! If it isn't, WHAT HAVE YOU DONE WITH HIM??!!!

"Hold up, Evie, it's me all right. I just got a haircut and shave. Do you like it?"

"This has got to be a joke. Where's my Adam?"

"Honest Injun, it's really me. Nobody would know how to find you or know your name if it wasn't."

"You look like an overgrown, sun-dried pear! And I think I preferred you, with all that hair. It just doesn't seem that I can trust you not to get into some kind of trouble or situation when we arrive at a new destination. The last stop you got lost for two days, before I located you. What's next?"

"Well, I have been thinking about some bone-lengthening, enhancement surgery to make me much taller," I jokingly replied.

"You're impossible. You need to be licensed to be out alone... But enough of your foolishness; we need to talk about what we found, saw and did today. Honestly, I'm now beginning to dread hearing what you might tell me."

And after an hour of our having something to eat and drink while he briefed me on what he did, he urged me to describe how my day's assessment went. Tired, but realizing this was our very last week for doing these accreditation surveys, I shook off the need to sleep and began my account.

One thing I knew all too well, after all these countless years of living with A.J., he had the capacity to get himself into situations far beyond what any mortal or immortal could or should. And I couldn't compete with him in that regard nor did I want or need to. A remarkable aura of good will enveloped his remarkable ability to do, say and become involved in uncommon, even outlandish, events. His decision-making process was based on the principle, best described as: "Yummy! Would you look at me?" I'm having the time of my life; each and every minute of it." It bears little resemblance to a deliberate, systematic and well thought-out process. Others may relish reading the classics, listening to a stirring symphony orchestra or tasting fine wine and exotic food. Instead, my Adam devours life; and his pell-mell, daily approach to it exemplifies this. And how, despite my often worrying over what might happen next, I love him dearly for it.

Thinking this, and despite my having the responsibilities of organizing both him and this survey on the planet we have so longed to return to, I decided during this last week to make an extra effort to describe my days to him with awe and wonder, rather than as a routine task. I so wanted this world to be successful and become accredited, as I'm sure Adam did as well. But my just looking around today, as I was driven from place to place, didn't fill me with an overconfidence that it would. There was something amiss; you could sense it.

And my goals today were to seek out those who were trying to be successful with respect to the Learning Standard, not just to find those who were floundering because of some shortcomings regarding poor learning opportunities or skills.

For most people to be successful at learning requires discipline and determination. Of course, there are certainly those to whom it comes naturally. Adam is a prime example of the former condition, and I am of the latter. His dyslexia has required that he continually struggle to capture and process new information and then desperately try to find strategies to retain and recall it. And that process has never gotten any easier for him. For me, learning is as simple as opening my eyes and ears to what's around me; and I remember everything I read, see, hear and feel. It's unfair, but that's the way it is. Every society and individual has to explore how to achieve their ultimate learning ability, despite the extreme polarity in learning abilities.

For my assignment on this first day of surveying, I wanted to explore what this world has learned since Adam and I departed it so long ago. To do so, I started with one of the finest repositories of this world's learning ability, the New York City Public Library System. I knew it would provide me with evidence of how well humanity had triumphed over ignorance and uncompromising dogma; while at the same time it would serve well to chronicle its openness to new ideas, freedom of expression and tolerance of debate.

During that inspection and afterwards, I would also be searching for individuals who have or were mastering various learning skills and sharing them with others. I wanted to hear from them how they plied their craft.

And finally, as that first night's discussion and review of the past day with Adam ended, I would describe to him my quick survey of public and private schools in The City to see how well instruction, analysis and comprehension were being taught and absorbed. I began first by describing my trip to the library.

I caught the Number 4 Bus soon after Adam left for Harlem, and within about ten minutes the bus driver announced that the 42nd Street stop was up ahead. (*see Appendix, "Manhattan Bus Map"*) As we approached it, I spied an immense building, which housed the New York Public Library, with the two lions, Patience and Fortitude, perched alertly on each side of the marble stairway leading to the front door. They gave one the impression that what was being sheltered inside was safe and precious; and that anyone was welcome, provided they respected a few modest preconditions for entry and use of its materials. And the size of the building, along with the atmosphere inside it, even without there being any posted reminders, made those expectations clear immediately: respect who and what is here, use faithfully what resides herein and have enough courage thereafter to dare to be a better person.

Immediately, my having already thought

about the approach I'd take once inside, I began my review of each of the major endeavors that has occupied this world since we were the last occupants here. They included archeology, paleontology, chemistry, physics, astronomy, zoology, botany, medicine, sociology, psychology, economics and all of recorded human history. As I have alluded to, I am a quick read, but even this assignment took me almost four hours to complete. And in doing so, it left me with an uneasy impression. Each new generation, humanity appeared to be leaving a heavier and heavier footprint on and throughout this world. It raised some questions and concerns that I had not expected to have, especially at this initial stage of our survey.

Reserving further judgment, from there I needed to explore where the most effective learning was occurring; which were the most effective methods to transmit this ability and how available was it to all humanity. But I didn't expect to get final answers to all these questions or solidify my impression as to any impact they might have or were making on this world today. That would only come after all ten Standards had been well reviewed by Adam and I this upcoming Saturday. For the rest of this first day, I needed to make two noteworthy forays. One was to check out representative institutions dedicated to learning, and the other was to spend some time with a few talented individuals who had established a firm grasp of a learned pursuit.

The first of these interviews was with an

individual who I found deep inside the stacks of the library. She was burrowed in a darkened area, sitting at a carrel, using only a small florescent light to shine down upon her scattered papers on a metal desk. She was hunched forward scribbling notes on an otherwise blank sheet of paper. Excusing myself, I approached her gently, not wanting to startle her. And as Adam has already mentioned, I also have a few extra abilities, one is that by my coming within a two foot radius of someone, I can put them at complete ease. And so it was with this individual.

In an almost whisper, I asked, "Would you mind sharing with me what you are writing, and how is it you are able to do so successfully?" As I asked this, I quietly pulled a chair up beside her from an adjacent, empty carrel.

Initially surprised at my close presence and questions, she then felt the accompanying reassurance that my presence posed no threat and she replied, "Certainly. I was at a point that I needed to stop anyway. I write mostly novels. And if things go well, I can write one or two books a year.

"The harder question to answer is 'how I do so?' And I'd say that one of the most difficult tasks in this process is deciding the story you'd like to tell and then how you'd like to bring it into focus. You then need to decide its format; whether it should be one that is sinister, romantic, fantastic, humorous, suspenseful, informative or possibly a combination of these. And let's say it is to be a humorous fantasy; can you be passionate about telling this kind of story, once you've made that decision? Do you have any personal experience with some aspects of the story? You must describe what you know and feel passionate about it. Without passion and involvement, the reader will sense your indifference and quickly lose interest.

"Choose a narrator or narrators carefully. They are the vehicle to move the story along. Give her, him, them or it space to expand, evolve, fail or succeed. And that should be the case for your original idea. As the story progresses, you must become involved and dedicated enough to it to let it flow naturally. You cannot be rigid about the sequencing of events or how the characters develop. If you resist this remarkable process, your story will become stale and the hidden mystery that is inherent in each one, even to you the writer, will never be revealed. And the magical quality of the work will be lost.

"Make a story outline or as I like to call it: a skeletal framework. The windows, doors, extra rooms and furnishings can be added as you move along in the actual writing. Then take each individual scene and study it, perfect it as much as you can in your mind before the actual composition begins. When it does, at that point you can include any research or key components. After all this, then begins the weaving process of actual writing.

"The writing must be done when your mind is at rest, no matter what time of day or night that is. The words need to pour out: this is the creative epicenter of the entire process. If you don't feel relaxed and at ease, your writing will reflect this and the reader will definitely know it. You might add anywhere from a single paragraph to 1,200 words to that individual scene in any one sitting. It all depends on how the writing process is flowing during those particular sessions. And flow they must. If they don't; wait!

"In between each scene you then have to develop the means to transport your storyline and characters to the next one. Whether this is in the past, present or future tense depends on what is occurring up to that point. Often this is the hardest part of the story telling, and it may halt your progress for some time. Be patient when it does.

"Most importantly, whenever you are thinking about the next scene, conversation, or transition; consider every option. And then try harder to think of another one. And finally try again. It is most likely that desperate lunge into the furthest reaches of your mind that will provide you with the best choice. Never... ever... select the first option that comes to mind. This is not supposed to be an easy process. If it were, everyone would do it. These decisions are the culmination of all your learning, experience and imaginative capability; and they are the central ingredients in your telling a story.

"Finally, keep the dialog and story straight forward. Move it along like you are having a personal conversation with the reader. Read it out loud to get a proper sense of the rhythm and pace.

You are, most of all, simply telling a story to someone."

Once she completed this brief description, I thanked her, and like Adam did, invited her to be at St. Patrick's Cathedral this Sunday at 4 p.m. I assured her that it would be well worth the effort. She simply nodded and turned back to her dimly lit sanctuary in the vast darkness of documented learning that surrounded her.

After I exited the library, I immediately caught the #104 Bus on 42nd Street and within minutes was dropped off at the Lincoln Center of Performing Arts. Somewhat disoriented, I had to ask a couple of people for directions before I was able to have someone point out to me which magnificent building in the sprawling complex was the Avery Fisher Hall.

Upon entering its lofty portico, I realized that my chances of finding the person I needed to speak with was unpredictable at best; but this venue was the best place I could think of to find the right one to seek answers to my question. Approaching the point of being almost overwhelmed by the cavernous auditorium, once I walked through one of its entrances, I knew there was nothing else for me to do but to plunge forward in my quest. As had always been the case in the countless other surveys that Adam and I had done previous to this last one, we somehow had always remained safe and steered in the right direction. Our destinations, whether generally to the various worlds or specifically to exact locations were seemingly selected for us beforehand; but that never lessened the mystery and nervousness of who we would meet or what the outcome might be.

And as I had hoped, sitting in one of the front row seats, in the orchestra section, was a solitary individual. It was almost as if he had been waiting for my arrival; it all seemed so prearranged. Not wanting to startle him, I spoke as I approached; my footsteps were almost completely muffled by the soft carpet covering the aisle way.

"Excuse me, sir," I said with a reverential hush, "Would you mind too much if I asked you a question? An associate of mine and I are doing a survey of Manhattan and your input is vital to its ultimate success. And certainly you are invited to the final summation of our findings. It will be given this Sunday at 4 p.m. in St Patrick's Cathedral."

Turning his head toward me as I continued my approach, which now placed me and him within my reassuring and calming radius, he replied, "How can I help you?"

In response to his invitation, I then ventured, "I was hoping that you might be a musical composer and that you could share with me how you begin developing a new composition."

There followed a lengthy pause, and then he spoke.

"Indeed I am, and at this moment it probably will do me some good to stop my fretting and return to the basics by trying to answer your question. It may give me the needed direction I am seeking at this time.

"To begin with, at least for me, a composition begins with being moved emotionally by an event, a vision, a lament or something that prompts me to want to express my thoughts and feelings musically. Unlike a story, which would be written to express any of these, a musical score is obviously created to be heard. Any comprehension of it by an audience is based solely on their ability to grasp my message through its melodic and harmonic composition. This work is not spelled out over some, 300-odd pages. With a symphonic composition, I have only a short time to capture them and then guide them through my interpretation of what I felt.

"And to begin this process, I start off with a simple melody or theme; a chorus if you will. And then I slowly build the complete score around that. It's that chorus that is at the heart of my message. All the various musical instruments in an orchestra serve to lift and guide the listener toward it from different directions or perspectives. This is done by using groupings of the string, woodwind, brass, percussion, timpani, and if appropriate, the supplementary instruments of the harp, piano and pipe organ. Because I hope and anticipate a widely diverse audience will eventually hear it, I try to offer multiple avenues to bring each of them along with me.

"The instrument of choice for me to begin this process is the piano. It offers the widest range of notes, chords and combinations of these of any instrument, with the exception of the larger pipe organ, which to me is unquestionably the ruler of all instruments.   Transcribing and blending this keyboard music with the other musical instruments for eventual orchestration comes only after I have accomplished composing a musical score on the piano.   And that could take months to years, depending on the depth or complexity of my feelings for the subject being explored."

Realizing that the maestro had much more important issues and demands facing him at that moment, within seconds after his explanation, I thanked him for his insights and excused myself. Hearing what he said convinced me that any culture that can devise instruments to play music, then compose, play and/or sing it, has taken a major step forward in the beginning to master the Learning Standard. And certainly those cultures, societies or worlds with a dearth of musical instruments and the music to play on them are indeed still in their formative stage.   Music not only enriches its citizenry, it confirms the likelihood of a general, overall maturity of its culture. But the music cannot be atonal in style or content. It has to have a melody, a quality of sound that enriches and inspires. And it has to be available for everyone in a given culture to play, sing or dance to. It has to celebrate life. Otherwise, it is simply noise.

Quickly, then, after again inviting the musical master to St. Patrick's on Sunday, I left the immense theater and hailed a taxi. Once I got inside one, I asked the driver if he possibly knew where I could find somewhere people went to have a good laugh.

Looking up at me in his rear-view mirror, he replied, "Lady, you've just asked the very person who knows the perfect answer to your question. Comedy acts are something I follow like others do their favorite sports team. And there is only one place close to here for you to go where you'll find it; it's a club devoted entirely to comedy, located on 44th Street. You'll get what you need there."

Relieved at his answer, I requested that he go there immediately, while adding that he should try to make time to be at St. Patrick's Cathedral this Sunday at 4 p.m. You could see he was puzzled by my invitation, but he politely and off-handedly agreed to try and come.

After paying my fare and leaving the cab, I entered the front door of the club and was confronted by a receptionist, sitting behind a counter. It confused me that this establishment had the appearance of a regular business, rather than that of a nightclub. Walking up to that individual, who peered at me over her reading glasses, I asked her if she would please direct me to the individual most likely able to know what it takes to make someone laugh. Sensing her reluctance and rising suspicion, I quickly leaned forward over the counter, separating the public from her work station, and allowed the aura of calm and cooperation to envelope her, and then awaited her reply.

"I'm sure you'll find what you're wanting, if

you speak with Ms. Styles. She's the funniest person I've ever met in my life, and she oversees this entire business operation. If you will, wait a moment; and I'll check to see if she's available."

And within five minutes I was being asked to sit in a small picture-filled room, with an individual who obviously seemed at ease. Sensing she was comfortable being who she was, her ready laugh at my request put me at ease as well. I hoped my quest for the last pinnacle of learning, to find and develop the best within you, was going to be addressed here. My question again, like with the previous two individuals I had just interviewed, was how does someone create refined humor, such as is associated with genuine, heartfelt laughter.

Her reply started with, "It must begin with a lifetime of learning how to confront yourself and your limitations. Only by beginning to know and to accept them will the wellspring of humor begin to surface. You have to lose a vaulted sense of yourself to find any true humor. So much of what is labeled as humor, e.g. sarcasm or cynicism being the most notable examples, is only marginally so. They are the lowest examples or forms of humor.

"I say that because they are usually generated by a sense of all-knowing, self-importance. They seem to arise from a judgmental or cynical reference point. Instead, the best examples of humor arise from self-deprecation or by the humorist or comedian ultimately being or becoming truly humble and non-judgmental. Unless you learn to minimize your own importance, the ever-tempting desire to direct your observations and comments at others' expense will result in humor that will always be second class.

"The greats in this business lose themselves in their best skits, monologues and routines; and they have learned to avoid focusing on the limitations in others. They direct their comments about events and impressions toward themselves. And to do this means you must continually be doing self-examinations. This ability is one of the most difficult of learned skills to master and to keep refining and updating. If you do it right, you are then able to make observations and report your findings about this ongoing self-examination to the public. And to perfect this loss of self-importance is the surest sign of a truly learned and potentially very funny individual."

Reflecting momentarily on what I had just heard, I then asked, "Can individual cultures or societies demonstrate this quality? Or to ask it another way, are there any cultures in which good humor is more prevalent than in others? And if so, why is that?"

"Certainly there are," she answered without hesitation. "And there are even times within a given culture that they may have a more lofty and prized appreciation and expression of good, quality humor. England, for instance, has consistently produced a society which, as a generalization, more frequently generates and celebrates genuine humor. And in the late 1940's, 50's and early 1960's this country had a stable of highly gifted humorists who entertained and inspired a generation of its citizens."

"Again, why is that?" I repeated.

"What can I say? Now you're probing at the very heart of any culture and its people. Why does anyone seem to mature when there are those in the same family or community who appear to become lost in elitism or indecision, self-doubt or aggressive tendencies?

"It takes self-discipline and honest, sometimes even brutal self-examination, to rise above snobbery, self-pity or anger. If any culture starts to become lazy, its habits become narrow-minded and self-centered; and more and more it begins a process of seeking to escape the present, forget the past and dread the future. Its individual and collective humor will fade, as sure as an unkempt bouquet of the brightest flowers will wilt. True humor, the kind that allows someone to see the desperately funny side of him or herself, is like an open window into that individual or culture. Optimism, fresh ideas and situations flow in and out of it. When it is closed, the individual or culture begins to wither. And the best of learning has disappeared."

Knowing that I had unfairly imposed myself upon this club's personnel and the individual who had shared with me her comments, I quickly made a mental note of what she'd said and excused myself after I invited her to St Patrick's on Sunday. I still had an afternoon to survey a sampling of public and private schools and universities to see what level of learning was occurring in each. And as with Adam's just-concluded day in Harlem, I was not ready to share with him any overall impressions or conclusions until our conference on Saturday, after we'd completed our surveys.

And besides, by the time I finished my review of the day with him, it was well-past midnight. We both had to get some sleep. The next day was reserved for Adam to perform the Caretaking Standard and me the Remembering one. Looking over at my eons-long companion, I could see his eyes were glazed over. Sleep was rapidly descending on him. And I, too, was exhausted. This day was officially over, and our very last accreditation survey had begun.

TUESDAY

SIX: THE CARETAKING STANDARD

Even with getting less than our usual amount of sleep that night, I awoke at dawn and was ready to head into the city streets by 6 a.m. Eve was right behind me as we twisted and turned our way out of the undergrowth surrounding our campsite.   She, likewise, had a full day ahead, surveying the Remembering Standard. Despite the various museums not opening until mid-morning, she had the uncanny ability to enter buildings whether they were locked down or not. That's my Evie for you...

And as soon as we came around the corner of the Conservatory Garden enclosure, we heard the honking of a car horn and looked up to see my three escorts waving happily at us.

"Over here!" Robert called out. "Come on! We're all ready to escort you through a new day of sightseeing. And who's this with you? IS THAT EVE? If it is, she's more than welcome to come along as well."

"Good morning," I replied less eagerly, not expecting nor particularly anxious that they would actually follow through with the offer to help me they had made the day before. Yet, in a way I was somewhat relieved to see them. It would make my navigating the various parts of the city far easier. But I was also worried that they might interfere with my trying to be as objective as possible. None of this inspection/survey business came easy to me. For Eve it seemed easier. She always seemed to flow in and out of social events and encounters with total strangers with much more dignity than me. She glides; I stumble and bumble. So, glancing over at her, I nodded toward the waiting cab to see if it was something she wanted to use.

"Sure thing, A.J.", she cheerfully acknowledged. "It will save me valuable time, if they can drop me off at the Guggenheim Museum and from there I can walk down to the Metropolitan Museum of Art, The Whitney Museum and The Museum of Modern Art. After that, I can then catch a bus back up to the Museum of Natural History and the Rose Center for Earth and Space."

"Ok, Hon," I replied, actually somewhat relieved. Seeing all the people and heavy traffic, even this early in the morning, made me a little skittish for her safety.

"You bet, Robert. Both of us will ride with you first thing this morning. Eve will direct you to where she wants to be dropped off; and I'll need to head all the way down Fifth Avenue to Washington Square, then over to La Guardia Place, and finally to West Broadway and White Street."

"You're headed to the 'Tombs'!" J.L. exclaimed. "There isn't anything else located on White Street. I know; my uncle was just paroled from there last week! We certainly know where that place is! But why are you going there, of all places to see and things to do in this amazing city? You sure have a strange idea of what sight-seeing is all about. What about the Statue of Liberty or Yankee Stadium? The Tombs! That's no place to visit. And I thought you mentioned going to Rykers Island yesterday. What changed your mind?"

"Going to the 'Tombs', as you call it, will make it possible for me to see more people throughout today. And none of this Eve and I are doing could or should be regarded as a 'visit'", I corrected, as Eve and I snuggled up tightly in the back seat with J.L. and Axe, with Robert sitting in the passenger seat up front next to J.L.'s father.

"What is this all about then?" Axe asked, leaning around to look at Eve and me. "Are you actually some kind of government inspectors? You're not from the City Social Services or Housing Department, are you?"

"Nope," I replied, smiling at Eve and winking. "We're doing a city-wide survey."

"What for?" Eddie, J.L.'s father asked, as he slowly pulled the cab away from the curb.

"To see if your accreditation can be renewed."

"Who's?" Robert interjected.

"Everyone's," Eve replied, finally entering into the conversation.

"Who is everyone?" Robert pressed, his voice beginning to sound a little tense.

"Any person living on this planet," she added.

"How often do you do this kind of thing?" Axe asked, with some amazement.

"All the time," I answered. "At least that is all we have done since our first assignment was completed."

"What was that?" Robert asked, sounding almost reluctant to do so, as if already skeptical as to what our answer may be.

"To foster life and at least insure rudimentary human habitation on any world we were sent to," Eve pronounced solemnly.

"Whoa, there…" Eddie said, as he pulled the cab over to the curb again and looked around at Eve and I me. "Are you saying that you somehow are responsible for giving birth to the first inhabitants of this world? Not only that, but that you have done this sort of thing on other worlds as well?"

"Yep," was all I said, looking proudly at Eve.

"And how often do you make these so called 'surveys', as you call them?" J.L. then asked, his voice filled with doubt and rising suspicion. And as these questions continued, Eddie reluctantly pulled the cab back into the flow of traffic.

"Up to now only one for each world; and this is our first one here," I clarified.

"When were you here last?" Eddie called out, pressing us a little further for answers.

"Approximately 550,000 years ago," Eve answered somewhat reluctantly.

Luckily, before the conversation became more confusing and confounding for everyone in the cab, excluding Eve, who always managed to weave her way through thorny conversations like this, while I became overwhelmed and even doubted myself what I was saying, she cried out, "Oh! Here's my stop. I recognize the museum by its unusual appearance. You can just let me out here."

Swerving over to a "Bus Only" zone and stopping suddenly like he was eager to discharge some half-crazed tourist, Eddie tried politely to ask, "Now are you sure you don't want us to meet you later for your next appointment?"

"No thanks," Eve replied, just after she reached around to give me a most-welcomed kiss and a poke in the ribs, as if to say, 'Don't divulge anything more to these fellows; they're already operating in an overload mode'.

"And I'll see you this evening, luv," she lovingly whispered to me as she slid out the door.

"Be safe out there, and have a good day, my dear," I replied squeezing her hand as she exited.

And then, as if relieved that one of their two crazy passengers had left his cab, Eddie accelerated and drove off, as if all his tires had just been changed on some premiere, formula racing car track, and he wanted to regain his lead. But he wasn't alone in that feeling. I was likewise relieved that the questions and any comments were ended for now. There followed a strained silence that signaled everyone was pondering the impossible, the ridiculous, the silly and as always happened when Eve and I have had these types of conversations on other worlds, the unthinkable.

In the meantime, I just laid my head on the backrest and immediately began to doze. I'm one of those people who can snooze while walking or even running. However, it was soon ended when Robert called out, "Well, here are the Tombs! Here is where you wanted us to drive you. And all I can say is that you've surely got to be some kind of foreigner. Nobody WANTS to come here to this place. This is a HAVE TO kind of place."

"Great!" I exclaimed. "Can you folks give me an hour or two? I'll meet you across the street at that coffee shop when I'm done."

An assortment of nods and guttural responses followed as I hurried out of Eddie's taxi and into the front door of the immense building that they called "The Tombs". Upon entering it, I was confronted with having to pass through a variety of security guards, checkpoints and finally a Reception Desk, behind which there was a fellow who looked like he did professional wrestling as his fulltime job. He was HUGE.

Walking up to him, I politely and fictitiously informed him that I was sent over by my parole officer to begin attending the early morning group session for repeat offenders. He briskly informed me that the session begins promptly at 6 a.m., and that I was late. Then he asked, "What's the deal? If you are on parole, why are you dressed like you are about to take a cruise to Bermuda or fly to Hawaii? Are you some kind of wise guy?"

"No, no," I tried to apologize. "It was just

all that I could afford."

"Where do you shop for your clothes? Who goes with you?... a travel agent? I can't wait to see what you are wearing the next time you come here."

"I hope today's session will be the only one I have to attend," I replied. "And if it is, you are invited to a special gathering this coming Sunday at 4 p.m. at St. Patrick's Cathedral."

"Why? Are you also a priest?" he mumbled as he turned away to answer an incoming telephone call. "Don't bet that you won't be returning. The characters who are in that meeting with you are in it for the long-term. But, if I'm in the area Sunday, I'll drop in to see what's happening. I'll have the family with me, and we're always looking for something new to see and do for a Sunday afternoon diversion. Now, take the elevator to the fourth floor. Your meeting is in Room 4012."

"Well, I can guarantee that if you do come, it will be more than just a diversion. Do try!" I added with some emphasis.

And after saying that, I quickly turned and raced over to the elevator. Within a couple of minutes, I found myself walking cautiously into a room filled with an amazing assortment of people. The chairs were arranged in a large semi-circle, facing a woman who must have been married to the fellow who sent me up here. She was almost as big as he was, but her voice seemed to purr. There was no shouting or yelling, as it turned out. It wasn't allowed. And if you successfully completed this class, your time of incarceration or probation was reduced. But make no mistake about it, in this room were more than a few people who would still have years left to serve out their sentence, no matter how much "good time" they earned. It was occupied at that moment by only "five-to-life" inmates.

With a simple nod, while only one of the maybe thirty men and women now seated before the counselor even bothered to look over to see who had just come in, I was given the distinct and clear directive to find a seat in the back row of the semi-circle of metal, folding chairs. She also gave the distinct impression that I was to pay strict attention.

I worked my way to the back, listening intently to the individual speaking and eventually to the next twenty-seven members of the group, making mental notes of what was said, how they acted and how those around them did. I wanted to report my findings and conclusions to Eve on Saturday, so I needed to remember everything possible.

During that next hour, the full range of crimes and loss of caring for oneself and others was described. These individuals had long-ago begun making choices that rejected any responsibility for themselves, to those around them and to the society they lived in. Their self-rejection matched what they sensed had happened to them by others around them and by the community at large. Their selfishness had become radicalized, and few of them gave me little hope of their wanting to change. They, along with society, perceived themselves as the worst of the worst. The air of hopelessness was choking. I was almost gagging when I saw everyone turn toward me, and I realized what the group facilitator had said after the last inmate spoke.

"It seems that today we have a newcomer," she noted looking directly at me. "Would you begin by telling us your name and then something about yourself?"

Clearing my throat, I tried to speak clearly and politely, given the grim circumstances surrounding this assembly of lost souls. "My name is Adam James… Smith".

"That's original," Ms. Oglethorpe, the group's moderator, rather snidely replied. "We try to be as honest as possible in here. Now try again. What's your real name?"

"That's it!" I said, probably a little too loudly for the occasion. "I'm the first person, ever, to be named, 'Smith'. Well, actually, maybe the second. My life-long partner and soon-to-become-wife chose it; so she probably was the very first. There were no others. Anywhere."

By then you could see Ms. Oglethorpe sorting through some papers on a desk behind her, probably trying to see if someone from the psychiatric ward had slipped into her early morning group by mistake. Finally, she turned back to me and replied, "Sure, and my real name is Eve."

"Oh, no mam; at least you're not the original Eve. She just got out of the cab I came here in a little while ago. She's on her way to survey one of your many, fine museums up in Midtown

Manhattan."

"Enough!" the once, soft spoken moderator yelled. "I won't have this meeting turned into a joke. Whoever your name is; why are you here, and what infraction of the law caused you to come here this morning? And why have you been allowed to dress like that? It's certainly not regulation, metropolitan-issue clothing. You are making a mockery of everything we are trying to accomplish. And as soon as this session ends, I will personally escort you down to the quartermaster to get regular issue, jail clothing. You are not leaving this building after this meeting. I'll see to that. Before this day is over, I'll get to the bottom of who you really are!"

"Well," I started, feeling that I'd better speak before she calls a guard to confine me or worse, "my first and really only crime, which in those days had not really been classified as such, was probably the worst ever recorded in the history of anyone on this planet. In all honesty, I should be considered The First Felon. But in my case, I wasn't sent to jail afterward. Instead, Eve and I were banished from Eden, where I'm sure if I hadn't done what I did, all of you here and all your relatives as far back as our own children would have always lived safe and peacefully in The Garden. You see, we are both from Eden, and I am the one who committed The First Crime...against all of humanity. No one here can even begin to match the sorrow and loss that I produced by my one, careless and selfish act."

"That is about the most ridiculous story I've ever heard!!" her voice boomed out.

But, to me, it was noteworthy that none of the prisoners said anything. There was no squirming and giggling. They all just stared at me. And it was at this point that I felt that a little extra persuasion was needed, particularly for the fuming moderator. Maybe, I thought, it might help curb her impulse to confine me, reduce the doubt in most and inspire others to alter their ways. So, deftly and without any hesitation I raised my arm again and pointed my fist toward one the far corners in the front of the meeting room. And immediately the silken, brilliantly white form appeared. And as she did, everyone gasped.

"It's ok," I announced. "No one is going to hurt you. But you can and should believe me. In addition, you can take with you today the knowledge and hope that if I could change and begin anew, after the awful crime that I committed, you can too. And any of you who can, please come to St. Patrick's Cathedral this Sunday at 4 p.m. for a very important meeting. And before I leave, I want to thank you for your honesty and patience with my story. I wish for each of you peace and a better life. Let it begin with your caring about yourself and then about others around you. You are still precious."

Getting up from my chair, I hurriedly left the room, as I had many other engagements to make before I rejoined Eve that evening. But as I got to the doorway, I turned and noticed that the White

Figure was still standing before the seated class. I thought they appeared to be listening to something. And not one of them had their mouths closed. Each one's jaws had dropped fully open, including their once-enraged, group leader.

As fast as the conditions would allow and was appropriate, I rushed through the Tombs, out its front door and across the street to the coffee shop across the street. And as you've probably already guessed by now, food and drink are not high on Eve's or my list of urgent, daily needs. After all, living as long as we have, there had to evolve some compromises with the usual daily chores and needs. We only ate or drank as the time or mood dictated, and it wasn't all that necessary to do either. But this morning I craved a strawberry milkshake, so I ordered one as soon as I entered the shop. Typically, it always seemed that no sooner had I taken my first glorious sip than there would be an interruption of my enjoying this favorite treat of mine. And sure enough, after I had, Robert dashed in the front entrance announcing he was sorry that they had been delayed; but there was a major disaster a few blocks from the Tombs. Traffic had been blocked for over an hour in every direction, and my escorts and driver were worried that I had been waiting a long time. I calmed his fears by indicating I had just completed my assignment and was ready for the next one, which as it turned out was going to the nearest hospital emergency room.

After he told me about the accident, I then became aware for the first time of ambulance sirens and immediately saw the first one rush past the shop window, heading north. Seeing this, I asked Robert what was the nearest hospital, and he told me it was Bellevue Hospital on First Avenue, northeast of us about eight blocks.

"We need to go there immediately!" I urged him.

"Why's that? You haven't been hurt have you?"

"No, but it's important that we get there as soon as possible!" I pleaded.

"Ok, you're The Man; and we want to try and get you safely wherever you want to go, but believe me, it's going to be difficult getting close to the hospital, what with all the emergency traffic heading in that direction."

"What happened to cause all these emergency transport calls?"

"I understand, from what we've heard on Eddie's dispatch radio, that there was a cave-in of some sort. Many people of all ages were trapped. Apparently, there was some construction going on above a subway tunnel. There must be a horrific struggle going on to save people just south of here."

"Then we must hurry. I need to get to that Emergency Room right away," I emphasized again.

And Robert was right, it was difficult for Eddie to maneuver through the traffic to get anywhere close to the hospital's Emergency Room. Realizing I couldn't get closer than two blocks away, I asked them to drop me off and meet me back there in two hours. Understandably, they were very reluctant to do so, having seen my directional skills the day before in Harlem, but I assured them that all I needed to do was follow the flow of emergency traffic right to the hospital.

And within five minutes, I was standing off to the side of the front door of the Emergency Room of the mammoth Bellevue Hospital complex and was confronted with a massive rescue response by countless ambulances and police vehicles. Injured and dying individuals of all ages were being transported to and then carried through its entrance way. There did not appear to be any shrouded, lifeless victims being ferried into the huge reception area. I could only assume this was because there having been a disaster apparently as large as this one that some kind of triage was taking place at the disaster site. And while there were occasional shouts, what immediately impressed me was the quiet deliberation and determination of those responders, medical personnel and even the relatives of the injured. It was as if everyone knew that hysteria, crying out or yelling would only hamper needed care. In this place calmness, selfless commitment and an unintentional heroism met this gruesome tragedy head on.

Eve and I have seen it over and over in the worlds we've surveyed. A remarkable few, and sometimes an even more remarkable many, come together to help rescue the injured, defy a wrong, halt a growing menace or combat a seemingly unstoppable evil. To them, duty is more than an obligation; it represents the sum total of these individuals' lifetime of caring and wanting the best for those around them. Here in this place, I saw individuals, families and a community working feverishly to save each other. Nothing can better define a society or a world.

I became so emotionally involved in what was happening that I almost automatically shifted, completely unnoticed, from a visible to an invisible bystander. It's the one ability I have; again far fewer than those possessed by Eve. But it, along with my one power of bringing forth Irene, my white silken archangel of mercy, to punctuate a message, manage a growing problem or bring hope and mercy to a situation, gives me an additional tool to address delicate or desperate matters during our surveys. With this one, I have always felt there was no situation that I couldn't ease into or out of, wherever I happened to be. And this day, in this place, I sense she would also be needed beside me.

I wandered, obviously unnoticed, from room to room watching the efficient pace of the personnel working on easing pain and suffering and saving lives. But in one room in particular I found two parents standing forlorn, looking down on a small child who obviously had been critically injured in the collapse at the construction site. It was painfully clear to me that life was ebbing out of her. And the parents were beginning to quietly sob, as they bent down over her.

Knowing that Eve and I have only a few directives to follow during our survey assignments, and one of the most stringent ones is that we are not to interfere with the ebb and flow of life on these worlds we are sent to, I still couldn't help myself. This was, as I have said, our last survey; and I could not stand by idly and let this tragedy play out before me as it was. I knew this would be another "apple-eating moment" in my life, but I kept telling the Upper Management that they should have chosen someone else to accompany Eve on these surveys. I'm hopeless.

So, even being invisible, if I hold out my closed fist and direct my arm in a particular direction, Irene, my ever-ready companion, will appear but only fully visible to those in the immediate area. And in this case I gave her quick instructions not to let this child slip away.

Now Irene is well aware of my checkered past and the tendency I have to push the limits of what is acceptable accreditation behavior. But she also has a streak in her that can shift into a co-conspirator mode. That's one of the reasons we get along so well. And with a simple nod, she understood and agreed with my request for her to help this family.

At first the parents of the child did not notice that Irene was standing behind them. Then as silently as she appeared, she deftly reached around the child's mother and laid her pale hand on the child's forehead. Without a word, the two parents turned toward the winged form and took a deep breath of surprise. Then, before they could recover and call out, Irene spoke, which oftentimes I do not get a chance to hear what is said. Today I did.

"Be calm," Irene began. "Your daughter will be ok now."

And just then the small form on the table took a deep breath and reached out both arms to stretch. She then opened her eyes and muttered, "Mommy, daddy…what happened?"

And with sobs of relief and gratitude, the parents embraced the child and turned to face Irene, who by now had joined me back in the invisible world of healing spirits.

"Nice work!" I said, as I finished my tour of the maze of emergency rooms and aid stations. "It's too bad, Irene, that this will be our last survey together."

"But probably none too soon, for you A.J.," she replied. "I think you asking me to do this last act will probably catch the eye of The Boss, and we may be in for some disciplinary action. I knew being assigned to you would get me into trouble; everyone told me so. But you know what?"

"What?" I asked, not too sure I wanted to hear her next scold.

"I wouldn't have missed it for all the rest and recovery I could have had not being assigned to you. You are definitely an unpredictable character, but your heart is good; even if you always seem lost and have absolutely no taste in clothes. What's next on your itinerary?"

"The Lower East Side Projects," I hurriedly replied, as the two of us hurried out the maze of hallways to the Public Entrance into the Emergency

Room reception area. "It's 10:30 a.m., and I've got to try and cover more territory. In other accreditation surveys that Eve and I have done, we had longer time frames, wider areas to survey and more opportunities to interview countless more individuals. Limiting us to this one island and doing the canvassing in only five days has severely hampered me in getting the widest response possible. I need to extend my own surveys somehow."

And as I regained my physical appearance once we were outside and Irene maintained her invisibility, but stayed beside me, she offered, "Why don't you have your escorts and driver distribute handouts? They could hand them out while you and I do our interviews."

"How would I get the results back?" I mumbled out loud, not wanting the many relatives and less injured pouring into the hospital to notice that I appeared to be speaking to myself.

"Have your four guides pick them up after they are filled out, use the internet or have a drop box located somewhere near your campsite I suppose," she suggested..

"Hmm. Let me think a bit on that. You may have cup up with something, Irene."

Within five minutes I was safely back in Eddie's cab and still puzzling over what Irene had suggested, when I spied Axe busily immersed, using a small device that was resting on his legs.

"Is that what is called a 'computer'?" I asked.

Turning to me, he answered off-handedly, "Of course. Where have you been?"

"You don't want to know," I replied with a deep sigh. "Can you write messages on it and then have them printed out?" I asked next.

"Sure thing," he answered. "All I need to do is type them and then go to a store that has a way to download and print whatever you want."

"Could they print a thousand of them?"

"I bet they'd be glad to."

"Do you have a computer address that they could be returned to, once someone fills them out?"

"Yeah, I do. Why?"

"Because I'm going to tell you what to write, and you'll get this first draft printed and copied. Later, once someone fills one out, it will be returned to you, sent to your computer address or placed in a drop box near where Eve and I are staying at night. You'll will then either print them out or give them to me early Saturday morning."

"That sounds like a lot of work," J.L. interjected.

"Yes, it will be," I agreed. "But he isn't going to be doing it alone. All four of you are to help him get the necessary supplies and paper to do this. It has to be done, and you're the only ones who I have to do it. And you'll be paid up front for any expenses and time spent.

"So then, that said," I continued, sitting down in the taxi's back seat without yet closing my door, "here's what I want you to type, as I dictate it. The heading will be:

<u>'Earth's Accreditation Survey Questionnaire</u>

(which was later changed to "<u>Adam's</u>
<u>Apples' Questionnaire"</u>)

Please answer the following questions truthfully. No one will EVER know you filled it out. Feel free to explain or clarify anything in the "COMMENTS" section below. Please send it by e-mail to the address below, hand it to the individual who gave it to you or place it in a large cardboard box behind the Conservatory Garden in Central Park by this coming Friday before 6 p.m. (One or more of the individuals handing them out will be there to protect them and later properly dispose of them.) Thank you for your time and the effort it will take to return it. Your participation and honesty in completing this survey is ABSOLUTELY CRITICAL FOR EVERYONE... EVERYWHERE.

QUESTIONS/ANSWER OPTIONS

<u>STANDARD:</u>   <u>OPTIONS: </u>
              NEVER
                    RARELY
              HESITANTLY
              FREQUENTLY
              ALWAYS

BEHAVING:
- -Do you have goals, dreams or aspirations?
- -Are you achieving any of them?
- -Are you able to cope with daily demands and challenges?
- -Do your feelings/actions help others?
- -Do your feelings/actions harm others?
- -What are your goals?

CARETAKING:
- -Do you daily find ways to help others?
- -Do you prefer to be alone?
- -Do you feel isolated?
- -Have you become disenchanted?
- -What have you contributed to others?

ADAPTING:
- -Are you feeling secure?
- -Do you welcome change?
- -When should you resist change?
- -What in particular do you find difficult adapting to?

AVOIDING/PROFITING FROM MISTAKES:
- -Are you in the trial and error stage of decision making?
- -Are you able to admit easily to mistakes or poor choices?
- -Are there fewer of them?
- -Are any, ones you need to ask forgiveness for?
- -What are your recent ones?

LOVING:
 -Do you love or have you been loved?
 -Do you believe you know how to love?
 -Could you pass the "Trust Test"?
 -What characteristics do you associate with being
      lovable?
 -What characteristics do you associate with being
      unlovable?

PROVIDE ANY COMMENTS IN THE SPACE BELOW

(E-mail address: adameve@accredit.uni)'

Once that was completed and we had driven to a nearby print shop and given them a request to print and make one thousand copies, I had Eddie drive me over to East 8th Street to the Projects. Next, I gave my associates instruction to return to the print shop and get the finished questionnaires and then the four of them were to come back here and each one go door-to-door handing out fifty questionnaires. They were to do the same at my next two visitation sites as well and then finally hand out one hundred each to scattered homes throughout Harlem sometime later this afternoon or evening. Doing so would use up the number of copies they were having printed today. And for the next three days, I suspected that I would have them print and distribute the same number of copies wherever we went.

The next two visitations went smoothly. I visited four families in the low income Sunrise Projects and ten patients in the Sunset Extended Nursing Facility on Roosevelt Island. In each location my team of distributors worked feverishly to get the questionnaires distributed over a wide swath within these respective compounds.

And by 3 p.m. they were able to drop me off at the United Nations so I could do a cursory review of the various care-giving programs administered by UN personnel. It was here for the first time, in all the accreditations surveys that Eve and I have ever done, anywhere, that I had the sensation that I was being closely observed, that someone was watching every move I made. And I sensed this was not any security operation. To me, as foreign as it all began to feel, I felt that it had no purpose other than to collect information, monitor my whereabouts, verify whomever I spoke with and, most significantly, begin to track me wherever I went thereafter. It gave me the disturbing awareness, the first since being ejected from Eden, of having to face the shadowy unknown and of it intending to do Eve and I harm. I knew then that our tour of this city was not going to be completed easily nor without great risk. And now I had involved these four innocent bystanders who were helping Eve and I.

With heightened anxiety, I finished my examination of the UN complex, hoping to get some idea of its world-wide accomplishments and capabilities, and by 5 p.m. I had Eddie drop me off at Madison Square Garden, where a political event was just getting started, with the President of the United States featured as the guest speaker. Scheduled to be discussed during this sizeable gathering of citizens from all over the Northeastern part of the country were the programs and goals set forth by this Administration to care for the nation's more neglected citizens. I wanted to hear and speak with as many people as possible about this before the President spoke and then hear what she had to say. And I had my four sidekicks pass out the same questionnaire at the four entrances/exits to over a thousand attendees. They were able to get more copies made while I was in the UN Building.

I sensed no threat once inside the auditorium, but when I came back outside and my team and I were heading back to Central Park around midnight, I could again feel we were being observed. And after I bid the fellows goodnight and agreed they could meet me again in the morning at 6 a.m., I quickly asked Irene if she sensed that we were under the same disquieting surveillance. Most disturbing of everything I saw or heard that day was when she said to me that she most certainly did.

My report later that same night to Eve was not as cheery as the night before. She applauded my use of the questionnaire and didn't dismiss my foreboding about being tracked. In fact, I sensed thereafter she had become very worried. Could it be that our final accreditation survey may come under attack of some kind? Were we in danger, and her prolonged silence after my description of what I sensed a confirmation of her concern? It just seemed too impossible to believe. Here, of all places.

SEVEN: THE REMEMBERING STANDARD

And because of this possible change in our welcome back to Earth, I didn't proceed right away with telling Adam how my day had unfolded. Instead, the two of us ate some fruit I had purchased and curled up for a while to sleep. A combination of pent-up exhaustion and worry lessened our eagerness to hear about the other's day. It wasn't until around 2 a.m. that I finally spoke and discovered that Adam had not been sleeping either. Realizing we both had another busy day ahead, we each took about thirty minutes to describe our second day's surveys. I spoke last.

I began with a brief description of the three museums that I visited: The Guggenheim, the Metropolitan Museum of Art and the Museum of Natural History and its satellite planetarium. I didn't visit a fourth one, after deciding I had garnered enough information from these three.

And, as I reemphasized to Adam that early morning, remembering is not a process of trying to be a slave to the past, nor is it simply a reminder of what cannot be left behind, as a society marches forward. There must be a balance between progress and tradition. We have seen over and over that evolutionary changes in almost every instance result in a struggle that may benefit a select group in some measurable way, but there are often spin-offs that inevitably have equally damaging consequences.

The museums I saw that morning elegantly remind anyone who visits them of the visual arts progression in this world's human history. And they also housed a growing and ingenious, 5,000 year old record of cultures that have preceded the present day. Likewise, before that distant time, there were fascinating displays and collections of priceless artifacts, fossils and bones, along with geological and cosmic objects that are filling in the canvas of time before and after the two of us were last here. Step by step, these citadels showed how this cradle, we call Earth, became stable and receptive enough to support life. And the dedication and scholarship to document this was remarkable and fascinating. Clearly, this world has and is dedicating vast resources to the cause of discovery and remembrance of its roots or beginnings. Its natural history is being well remembered and stored for safe keeping.

But what is not being remembered and documented as well are the tragedies, defeats, losses and social upheavals that have marked this progression of life. After viewing these three museums, I was left needing to find evidence of how or who is remembering and recording the byproducts of change. What emphasis or remembrance is being placed on tradition, on timeless values, on our Creator and Lord, on the common woman or man or on the struggles, defeats and victories in this process?

Is life now better for more or fewer people? When liberty or freedom comes, does it give people more or less hope? Is there evidence that newly freed individuals and cultures become responsible after its advent? Only then does freedom of any kind benefit a society. Is the pursuit of happiness closer or fading further for more or less people? Are the social changes occurring now, e.g. exploding legal and illegal drug use; single parent households; secularized, even elitist, reforms discarding some valuable traditions, resulting in a better or a more painful life for far too many?

What is this planet remembering? More importantly, what is it forgetting along the way in its struggle to preserve life in a post-Eden world? History is not a drab and boring enterprise. It is another mirror that each society must look in to. It has to be placed alongside the one that gives each of us an image of our present day's grooming and fitness. It tells us what lies beneath the external image in that second mirror. It's filled with our collective memories and remembrances. It's who we really are. And the more we forget, deny or ignore, the less we are now. There must be a balance between change and remembering, between innovation and tradition, between those who have so much and those who have so little. The more selfish and insulated a society becomes, the easier it is to slip into despair and rebellion.

Adam then leaned up on one elbow after I had expounded on all this and asked, "So, what did you do then… after coming up with all that?!!"

"I decided that I needed to go to two major groups of institutions to continue this particular survey."

"Un huh," he mumbled, sleepily. "Which were?"

"Three religious centers or theological seminaries and to two major, national news outlets."

Then continuing my review of what I did the day before, I explained to Adam that I went to two separate theological graduate schools at the upper end of Broadway Avenue. One was primarily a Christian, non-denominational institution and the other was a Jewish one close by. And with a little slight-of-hand, I was able to convince the Deans of both schools that Adam and I were somewhat special guests who had recently returned to New York City for a special purpose. There was more than the expected, under-whelmed response to my initial introduction, but that soon turned to the same usual stunned shock when I disappeared and then reappeared dressed in the clothing we wore in those much earlier times, sporting a clump of branches that we would have been gathering for firewood.

I kept that transformed appearance until a General Assembly was called and all the faculty and student body in each institution were hurriedly gathered together, and I began to address them. At that point, for a little extra drama and to convert any lingering doubters, I disappeared again and reappeared dressed as Adam and I are now for this current survey.

Having their undivided attention, I then asked for the audience to please calm themselves and focus entirely on what I ask them and on their most candid and honest responses. Further, I noted that I did not want to see any camera flashes or any recording devices nor notice any idle conversation amongst any of them. Their focus had to be entirely upon me and on what I said and asked. My time was far too short and valuable to be wasted on theatrics and publicity.

I then proceeded to ask them three questions and added that I would choose five responses to each question from various people who raised their hands scattered throughout the audience. Once selected, they were to stand and speak clearly and succinctly. I noted that I did not want any rambling or anyone trying to impress me. I emphasized that all I was looking for were truthful answers.

My three questions were: What role does tradition have in their training and subsequent ministry? How do they describe their belief in God and then plan to relate that same belief to their parishioners? And finally, do they, amongst any other eventual duties that they may have, consider that they will become the custodians of remembrance; and why or why not?

After my asking these questions to each of the three assemblies that I stood in front of that afternoon, there always followed a brief period of silence. I say brief, because with some heightened emotion and insistence I followed up by yelling, "I need answers NOW!! This is not some idle exercise. Much depends on your answers… much more than you could EVER imagine!!" And after that outburst, all three audiences were very cooperative and informative.

The third religious center I went to, because of its location close to the vast media broadcast centers adjacent to or along the Avenue of Americas, was an Islamic Center, which included a Mosque and a school for religious training. And after getting the attention of the various elders and students there, I asked them the same three questions.

"I bet you made a particularly unique and lasting impression on those young minds and their professors today," Adam interrupted. "Talk about history appearing suddenly at your doorstep and then it demands that you pay undivided attention to the sacrifice and labors of the countless contributors to their heritages and daily comforts. It probably would have paralyzed me."

"You would hope it did, wouldn't you," I answered, before hurrying on to describe my last set of meetings that late afternoon and evening with two major broadcast outlets. And once I gathered the corporate leadership and news crews and announcers together in each building, I asked them to answer the two following questions in detail. And of course, because of their professional mandate to be doubters and the ingrained need for confirmation, I did my usual disappearance, transformation and retransformation before each of the two audiences.

"What were the questions you asked them?" Adam interrupted me.

They were lengthier than the ones for the religious training students and their faculties. The first was: "What percentage of the population, nationally and internationally is recalling past tasks, lessons, experiments, theories and then fashioning or exploring new ideas, developing new material or approaches to improve their own daily lives and those of others, thereby extending the known or knowable boundaries for everyone?"

And the second question was: Amongst those who are not aged nor seriously ill, is the percentage of the population both nationally and internationally increasing that is less able or willing to recall, whether due to multiple excuses, drug use, laziness or indifference and then deliberately ignoring and violating accepted laws and customs of human behavior? In other words, is this world becoming more forgetful and violent, whether due to revenge, cruelty, avoidance, laziness, extremism or escape? Is the non-aged population becoming less able or willing to develop or recall significant and life-altering memories? And would they rather live only for the present moment?

"What did everyone say? Adam then chimed in.

"You'll have to wait until our discussion on Saturday to find out," I sleepily replied. Right now, it's way past time for us finally to get some sleep."

"Did you invite anyone you talked to about coming to hear us on Sunday?"

"Yes, I did. Everyone I spoke with today was invited."

WEDNESDAY

EIGHT: THE ADAPTING STANDARD

I awoke the next morning feeling like all my body weight had been transferred to my head. I couldn't keep it upright. My chin kept falling on my chest. And my arms and legs wouldn't move. All I could do was moan. If this hadn't been our last survey, I would have had to tell Eve that at least it was mine. You've got to give me some slack, though. Being over 550,000 years old has to allow you some. And it was damp and chilly besides. Sleeping under bushes and trees is far from ideal, particularly when we were surrounded by luxury apartments and condos. And even though I am writing this report on Saturday, it still disturbs me to think of all the nights, over 200,750,000 to be more precise, that Eve and I have not been able to sleep on a mattress, in a queen size bed; it being supported on a thick-pile carpet, covering a sturdy, hardwood floor. Grass, leaves and twigs have been our mattresses for all these years, and don't think I don't have a raging case of arthritis, because I do.

But, Eve, bless her heart, never complains. And that makes me feel even worse. She's a battler. I was born wounded, and I don't let anyone forget it. I think that sometimes all she needs to do is blink her eyes five times, and she's refreshed and ready for the next day. And she never looks frumpy. I define the term. And my holiday attire is beginning to look the part as well. Soon enough, I'm not going to be able to enter any public building without Irene leading the way, trying to shroud me all the while.

But mustering some strength from the depths of the unknown, I mumbled to Eve, "We'd better head out to the street and see if the fellows are there yet. I'm sure they'll give us both rides today, at least to our initial destinations. But it wouldn't surprise me, if they don't show up. Yesterday was a real strain on all of them, I could tell. I had them racing door to door with those handouts, and then I wanted them to make sure the same was arranged for handing them out in Harlem today by some of their trusted associates."

"Oh, I bet they'll be there," Eve called out, in her amazingly irritating, early morning, lilting voice. "They are a fine crew. How they ever agreed to assist you I'll never understand, but you always seem to have that knack. Everywhere we've been, you seem to attract a band of helpers. It must be the helpless aura you radiate."

"Nice, hon," was all I could mutter in

response to her often surgical observations of me.... "Anyway,' I continued, "we need to hurry up and see if they are outside waiting for us. Otherwise, we'll have to get on shank's pony to get to our various destinations. Luckily, for me, if that's the case, I plan on being in one place all day today."

"Where's that?"

"Grand Central Station."

"Well, I've got a day like you had yesterday."

"How so?"

"I'll be going to at least four different locations, most scattered far from each other. It's the only way I can get a reasonably good assessment of the Sharing Standard for this world. But I do like your idea of circulating questionnaires. I'm just hoping my standards will be universal enough that I can avoid doing that. You got the tougher ones this time. Or at least you have the ones that on this particular accreditation survey, one which limits us to such a small geographical area, are probably best surveyed with additional input, beyond your personal observations and interviews."

"That was kind of my thinking as well. But for now though, we'd better hurry. Sun's up. It's time again to see what makes this planet's occupants tick."

And sure enough, once we cleared the underbrush and tree line, there parked right adjacent to our campsite was Eddie's cab and the four fellows standing beside it. Oddly, they waved and called out to us like we hadn't seen each other for a couple of years. I found myself really getting attached to these fellows. They had nothing to gain from helping Eve and I. We certainly couldn't pay them much. We were only given enough money to make expenses. While it's true, we could put in a good word for them to Irene and her fellow travelers and messengers, but beyond that our instructions were very clear. Make no promises or guarantees. Just report your findings, once you've made the survey. And interestingly, it didn't seem to matter to these fellows that we didn't appear to offer them that much. They seemed to sense that. Street smarts, I presumed. They possessed something that was becoming progressively evident to me; something that was particularly unique to this world: it was a surprising and unpredictable goodness.

Eve called out "Good morning" in her most cheery voice, while I continued to fumble with tucking in my sport shirt and getting my sandals on correctly. Rushing up to them, I blurted out, "Do any of you know of a band that I could hire for today. I need to have some music to attract a crowd."

"Does that mean we don't have to pass out more of those sheets of questions, like we did yesterday and now have our relatives doing the same today around our neighborhood?" Robert briskly asked.

"No, it doesn't," I answered, although wanting to acknowledge my gratitude for all they have done and are doing. "Unfortunately for you, we'll all still need to distribute them periodically at the various entrances and exits of where we are going today. But we also need to get the attention of folks to stop by and speak with me. I felt a little music might do the trick."

"Well, look no further," J.L. announced, rather proudly. "We have our own little band."

"Who does?" I asked, surprised.

"The four of us. We play calypso jazz. Our family all migrated here from Jamaica, and we were taught how to play from an early age. Even Eddie plays with us. He's our saxophone player. I play the electric guitar. Axe, here, plays the drum set and Robert plays the steel pans. How about yourself? Do you play anything?"

"As a matter of fact, I do," I acknowledged, but very surprised at what I had just heard. "I like to play the harmonica."

"Great!!" Robert shouted. "We can bring along one of our extra amplifiers and you can wail along with us."

"Does your band have a name?" I then asked, trying to control my mounting excitement.

"Not really," Eddie interjected. "It's something we've toyed with for some time, but nothing has really stuck."

"Well, then, I have a suggestion. I think we should call it, 'Adam's Apples'!".

Each of the four looked at one another and quickly concurred; and almost instantaneously, "Adam's Apples" it became. But then after Eve and I got in the cab, along with the four others, we had to head back up to Harlem to get their equipment. They kept it in a small trailer that could be hitched behind Eddie's cab. And after a little rummaging around, they found an extra amplifier for me to use; along with an older model harmonica with the necessary adaptor attachment.

And by 7 a.m. we were heading down to Wall Street to let Eve off for her first assignment. And by 8 a.m. we had set up "Adam's Apples" in front of a vacant ticket counter on the Main Concourse of Grand Central Station. But this was only after I had Irene do a little diplomatic intervention with the security and management personnel assigned that morning to the Station. She had to convince them we were not there strictly for entertainment. And even with her supernatural and hypnotic powers, we were only begrudgingly allowed to play for that one day. One can never underestimate the resistance to change found in some civil service employees.

Just before we arrived at the Station, I had Eddie stop by a print shop and we had more handouts and a banner made that we stretched out over us, just above the old ticket counter windows. It announced to all the passersby:

"STOP, LISTEN AND CHAT. ALL QUESTIONS ANSWERED HERE... AFTER WE ASK YOU A FEW. ONLY HONEST ANSWERS WANTED. MUSIC COURTESY OF 'ADAM'S APPLES'."

Our location was perfect. In front of us were the Stations' Information Booth and the huge four-faced clock, and around them swirled thousands of commuters, travelers, tourists and what appeared to be people I later came to call "the lost". And after we played our first two selections, with me even having a solo part, there was a steady flow of people, either stopping to pick up a questionnaire or wanting to speak with us. It wasn't long before my playing time became very sporadic.

Eventually, each of us "Apples" ended up taking turns cruising through the massive building distributing the handouts or positioning ourselves at one of the entrances to hand them out. And by noon we had handed out all the ones we had printed earlier that morning. Also, by that time I was beginning to form a fairly good impression of what the major issues were which allowed people either to adapt to this world around them or to those which hindered it. Any summation, however, would have to wait until Saturday. I was just too busy enjoying myself... at least during the first part of the day.

What I can say was that tops on my list of things that impressed me about the countless people who came up and freely and openly discussed their concerns about adapting was the obstacle of living in a culture whose changes were increasingly speeding up. And it was only getting faster, through what they described as all communication becoming almost totally "wireless". This evolution in their technology was forcing people to spend less and less time in physical contact with one another and was bringing about an increasingly stronger sense of separation or isolation. This technology seemed to me to be a potential hazard for everyone; because in my view, adaptation to change requires the supportive network of a community one can touch, see and hear. .

In addition, I noted that for most people, all of them far, far younger than me, this change was becoming daunting and possibly even terrifying to them... if they had time to admit to it. I saw this emerging fear within all the various cultures I met that day. New York, after all, is The Melting Pot; and I had a chance to meet people from everywhere.

And there was something else about the unparalleled pace of change that caught my attention. It seemed to me the faster the changes, the more indentured people became to some authority or power beyond themselves; and that Authority or Power was becoming more of a concern to me. From everyone's descriptions, it seemed to be radiating from a body that could only be described as The Elite Ones.

Likewise, it was about this same time that I began again to have a sensation, which was then even stronger than what I had the day before; and it was all too familiar to me. It occurred on the very day that Eve and I were banished from Eden; it was that of absolute threat. Indeed, it was again the threat of the unknown, of the unknowable and of mortal danger. After that first experience with such a feeling, it took me eons to regain a state of mind that was gleeful and that welcomed the opportunities of each new day. Instead, for years, I became introspective, full of grief and shame, and was almost paralyzed with fright. Those same feelings were now emerging again, but this time there had been no eviction, no transgression on my part or Eve's; at least as far as I was aware. Something external, for the first time in our lives, was stalking me, and possibly Eve, but I didn't have the sensation that Eve was the central focus of my premonitions. I sensed something terrible was afoot, and it was only the noise, scurrying around of thousands of commuters and visitors in that mammoth hall that prevented me from feeling a more tangible threat. Suddenly, my tendency to silliness, pratfalls and jolliness seemed senseless and distracting.

I knew we were getting the information that I needed to complete the summation of this Standard, but when I became aware of how much around me and Eve was probably being manipulated by The Elite Ones, a great sadness overwhelmed me. I was becoming frightfully aware that multiple sets of eyes were focused on me, and that they were tracking me like I was some kind of prey. It made me shudder. Why here? Why on a world we left so many thousands of years ago? Why now? Why after all the many worlds that we had been privileged to initiate life in and then later return to certify their continued occupancy, did we now face such resistance and threat here?

Brushing aside for the time being these forebodings, I urged us to continue our performances, which at certain times attracted hundreds of listeners and onlookers. "Adam's Apples", minus me, performed; and I quizzed and studied the various reactions of countless people throughout the rest of the day. And for once, we finished before nightfall. By sunset that day, I was back in Central Park taking a nap when Eve woke me for dinner. That night we decided we were going to a restaurant to eat. It was always the one special treat we had during our time of doing these accreditation surveys. Being with Eve that evening allowed me to forget the misgivings I had been having. I began to think later that night that I was again being silly. It probably had to be my advanced age and my inability to quickly adapt anymore to circumstances. But, unquestionably, this had to be our last survey. I was getting too feeble to do this any longer, and I knew it. Eve did as well. I was old enough. Still, before I finally went to sleep that night, a feeling of mystery and danger swept over me. I shuddered, snuggled closer to Eve, and fell deeply asleep.

NINE: THE SHARING STANDARD

For the first time since I can remember, after Adam's description of what he was experiencing, coupled with my own premonition about being watched, I was nervous about what the future held for us. He and I were given remarkable abilities; that's obvious to anyone reading this account. Living and traveling as we have for all these years and with Irene being Adam's vigilant aid-de-camp, there is no reason for us to feel anything but special and privileged. But like we've said, this was our last survey; our duties were finally ended after this one. We could look forward to finding everlasting reassurance, peace and love in the arms of our Eternal Creator. We would be going Home at last.

Just the same, I wasn't prepared, nor do I imagine that my happy-go-lucky mate was either, for a sinister and stalking presence to hound us during this final mission. It's so out of the ordinary from all we've experienced before. Why here? What's so different about this world? I could only think that maybe today or tomorrow's surveys might uncover a hint of who or what might be behind this potentially harmful threat.

So with that somewhat reassuring thought in mind, I kissed Adam and bid his "Apples" a successful day, as they let me off at the New York Stock Exchange building. Employees were already rushing inside the marble entrances, outlined so dramatically by the immense American flag hanging above them. There was an unmistakable hustle and scurrying about with these undoubtedly successful eager and bright couriers of the world's capital. They were the tip of the spear that cleared the way for the massive movement of money, goods, services and eventually people, the world over.

Despite what I can only gather with what I've found out thus far in my inspections, and might possibly have confirmed with this day's, the apparent dramatic slowdown of this country's economic engine and a seemingly irreversible loss of much of its middle class due to a continental-wide evacuation of its manufacturing and intellectual property and spirit, these individuals who are spiriting ahead of me into this building appear immune to these reverses in this country's fortune and promise. They seemed to me eager, well-fed and very flush with success; the entire world has become their financial playground.

I circulated in and amongst these brokers, bankers and financial wizards for the next three hours, speaking with all levels of management and floor staff. And by the end of that timeframe, I had an unsettling, but well-focused appreciation of the local, national and international exchange and selective accumulation of treasure worldwide. It appeared to represent a form of sharing that was becoming grotesquely selfish and selective.

However, I didn't have time to dwell on what I was then hearing and seeing; it was time to move on. Once outside, I quickly hailed a taxi and was taken to the Red Cross Office and Family Respite Center on 28th Street; its location being just north of Madison Square Park. Luckily, I was still able to be driven there quickly; it still being in Lower Manhattan.

And even though it was not the national headquarters for the American Red Cross, I still was able to get an unmistakable confirmation of the benefits and contributions to and by millions of people everywhere through and to this organization. Its reach locally, nationally and internationally was impressive; and the dedication of its staff and the volunteers was heart-warming. Before I left there, they directed me to check out another volunteer organization that had a local, national and global impact: The Habitat for Humanity. These two associations and others like them renewed my hope of what people around this world can do when they are able to give of themselves.

From these investigations, I hurriedly made

my way to various food banks, thrift stores and church basements, looking for other ways that people share with one another. And that afternoon was spent interviewing three philanthropic foundations, two large cooperatives and a large complex that held military recruiters for each of the Uniformed Services. Finally, as late afternoon was approaching, I ended this most frantic day interviewing a dozen residents in various Park Avenue Apartments, each located not too far from our campsite in Central Park.

When I did get back to where we were bivouacked, I found Adam fast asleep. Not wanting to wake him immediately, as I had been observing how exhausted he had been appearing lately, I set about scribbling down a few notes about today's interviews and my observations. I thought later that evening we would go out for our special dinner at a nearby restaurant I discovered on my way back from the interviews in the apartments. In the interim, this gave me time to collect my thoughts about what I observed today.

And at that point I did have some initial observations about this Standard that I would be discussing with Adam on Saturday. My summation and final grade would have to wait until then. But, to summarize what I found, let me say first that without question there is a resilience and generosity in these ancestors of Adam and I. And it made me very proud to see how dedicated and determined so many citizens of this city were to help others by sharing their time, money and talents. They, undoubtedly, are the promise and visible hope for this world; one that as I have noted previously, now worries me greatly.

However, there is a flip side to this generosity and goodness, and I saw it all too clearly. I couldn't help but wonder, what is this all about? Because it appears from the interviews that I conducted today and the research I did on Monday at the New York City Public Library that there has been a significant shift in the distribution of power and wealth throughout this world; a place that is so important to Adam and myself.

Even during the times he and I were last here, we saw the development of tribal leadership and the rudimentary beginnings of accumulating whatever was most valued at the time, e.g. salt. Then, as I have recently read about, after we departed this world, there began to develop city states, with a warrior class being chosen or elevating themselves into leadership roles. And wealth became more centralized in their hands. Sadly, the next step in the progression of centralized power came in the form of regional conquests, as seen by the Persians, Greeks, Romans, Mongolians, Chinese and Mayans. And, as always before, the wealth of conquest continued to accumulate solely within the conquering class, with only modest benefits being extended out to a chosen few of their most trusted lieutenants. There was no other hierarchal distinction for the remainder of the people in these cultures. Left faceless and penniless were the serfs, slaves or soldiers and their families.

It was a two-tier world for centuries.

Subsequently, two developments began to emerge during and immediately after the so-called Dark Ages that began to alter, somewhat, this bleak picture for the vast majority of this world's population; the rise of religion's role in the various cultures, particularly in Europe and the Middle East and the emergence of merchants and traders. Mercantilism and commercialism began competing for influence and power throughout the world. But absolute power was still held by the individuals and families of the warrior class, i.e. the kings, queens, emperors, high priests and generals. However, throughout all this period the outreach and power of any given kingdom or religion was limited either geographically or militarily. There was never any single warrior or religious leader who conquered or ruled the entire world and its occupants. And throughout this timeframe, there were only a smattering of individuals beyond these sets of leaders who had privileges above or beyond the mass of citizens: they were members of the priesthood, the imams and the merchants.

Then came the long-awaited, needed change for this world; the development of democratic governance. It was to decentralize power into the hands of elected officials. Although, it was a slow and painful process taking any of it away from the warrior and religious monopoly. Now politicians were assuming the roles of leadership and privilege in scattered regions of the world. And along with that remarkable change began the agonizingly slow advent of a middle class, which owed its rudimentary beginnings to industrialization and increased trade within nations. No longer were there just two tiers in a society. And the wealth of a nation began to be more evenly distributed throughout its citizenry. The wealth of the warrior-class aristocracy was being slowly redistributed, along with its previously held all-encompassing powers. Citizens rose up in revolution. Sometimes it was violent and sometimes it was relatively peaceful. But each time there was usually a politician rather than a warrior or religious figure in a leadership role.

Then another development occurred within the last century that again began another shifting of power and privilege. It was the development of student testing to determine one's intelligence and potential. And the results of these tests would often determine where and how far a particular individual might rise in a given culture. These tests were to determine who eventually would merit the rewards of a culture... even in a democracy. They became the litmus test for someone's future power and privilege. And more importantly, as time went on, this same privilege began to be passed to their offspring. It was a case of the most valued members of a culture becoming united and passing their legacy, privileges and connections onto their children, who now also scored highly on the admission tests to the most privileged institutions of higher education.

And finally there emerged out of this new

class a sense of entitlement, snobbery and elitism that caught the various cultures worldwide by surprise. It became centralized in the university, financial and corporate institutions, and the result has been the rise of a new global-wide ruling class.

As a result, for the first time in the history of humanity an entity has blossomed that is borderless and all-encompassing. Globalization, as most easily recognized by its corporate base, has become the de facto ruling body of this planet. Borders, political affiliations, religious influences and ninety percent of the population are falling victim to this takeover. A two-tiered world is reemerging: the very rich and powerful on one level and the often victimized remainder of humanity on the other.

It is no benign secularization that is taking place. Nor is it a "free trade" nirvana. It is a metastasizing process that serves The Elite Ones, as Adam calls them; and it has the very real potential of killing this planet.

'To combat it, I see pockets of heroic individuals struggling to make their contributions to counteract the abuses of arrogance, power and centralizing wealth. The only hope left for this world in this regard is for them to rise up, speak out, come together and resist this economic and self-perpetuating takeover. Adam and I have to somehow help them with a plan. The sharing of wealth, privilege and all goodness that makes humanity so special must be redistributed and revered. This global manipulation must be stopped… somehow.

THURSDAY

TEN: THE AVOIDING/PROFITING FROM MISTAKES STANDARD

Our evening out was swell. Now that we were more than half way through this survey, we could take a deep breath and relax a bit. Soon our extended lifetimes of birthing, nurturing and assessing were soon to be transformed. We had no idea how or what would happen once we completed this assignment. But, of course, we never knew where we were headed once we finished the one just completed. We just woke up the next morning in a new location, with new directions and a new mission to complete. But not after this Sunday night's sleep. And our wish list seemed endless, as we chatted about the possibilities for our future.

Being "on the road", so to speak, for all these years has left us feeling more or less like shipwrecked survivors on an endless journey to find land, be rescued or find a haven where we will be safe and dry. However, never you mind, Eve has been the captain of our drifting scow. I've just tended to its sails and bailed water when necessary. Her coming into my life was such a blessing for me. Without her, the loneliness would have no doubt driven me mad, if I stayed in Eden or lived anywhere else.

But before I could finish this bit of reverie, I was nudged back to the present by some rustling in the bushes to the west of us. Eve spun around and whispered to me, "Who could be coming this way so early in the morning?"

"I don't know," I whispered back. "Only the fellows know where we are, but even they don't know exactly where."

And suddenly, Robert burst through the undergrowth, excitedly exclaiming, "We are sorry to barge in like this, without announcing who we were or why we're doing this; but we felt it necessary to stop you before you left your campsite."

"What's the matter?" Eve exclaimed, shocked to see all four of our assistants come fully into view in our refuge area.

"We've been having growing concerns for your welfare," Eddie announced. "I'm sure you probably are sensing it as well; most likely you have even before us. But each of us has become increasingly aware that one or both of you are being observed when we are out in the general public. We don't think whoever it is has any idea where you have been sleeping, but we've decided we're not to be consistent where or when we pick you up or drop you off."

"We want to keep you safe!" J.L. blurted out. "Ok! Ok!" I exclaimed, struggling to become awake enough to put some calmness back into the growing panic. "Eve and I have also noted some unusual behavior as each day has progressed, almost like someone is following us, or more specifically, me. It may not be anything to worry about, but it is a first for us. Never before have we experienced this kind of behavior; if, in fact, what we are sensing is real. That said, your precautions are much appreciated; and we'll be glad to accompany you along a different route in and out of here. Would you agree, Eve?"

"I guess so," she replied. "It's just so highly improbable that something threatening could be afoot. It's not like we are challenging anyone… yet. No one, not even you four standing here, knows what is to be the outcome of our surveys. In fact, neither are we. We aren't done. We haven't even finished our investigations. And wherever we've done these surveys before is so far removed from here that no one could conceivably know what's at stake."

However, it did occur to me while Eve was saying this that there was no way we could know for sure that someone or something might not have divulged in some mysterious manner the purpose of our being back in this world. It seemed highly unlikely, given the distances we travel from one inhabited world to the next for these surveys. And yet, deep down inside the depths of me, there was this nagging premonition of great danger and threat.

"It's settled, then," I announced. "Give us a few moments, and we'll be ready to accompany you out of here."

Still shaken from their sudden appearance, Eve and I looked at each other with some alarm and then reached out to one another for the reassurance that we had to have to continue our work here. Don't get me wrong. I am not a brave soldier. Anyone who lives as long as I have has learned to dodge danger masterfully. I would like to be, but I'm not; and I know it. If it is any consolation, I recognize it in others immediately; and I salute them enthusiastically for it. I might have some other worthwhile traits, but bravery under fire is not one of them. Luckily for Eve and me, the "Apples" appear to have it. How fortunate we are to have them as our guides and guardians. Irene has usually been enough of a presence to protect us. But, somehow, I sense even she is perplexed and worried about our safety.

Anyway, with these unsettling thoughts, we finished dressing and wove our way out of the underbrush and onto a pathway that began to lead us over to Central Park West, the street bordering the western edge of Central Park.

Through some twisting and turning and led by our four companions, we eventually circled around the "Great Hill", as they call it in these parts, and came out to where Eddie's taxi cab was parked on the corner of 105th Street and Manhattan Avenue. From there, we immediately drove Eve to an entrance into Columbia University on 118th Street and Broadway, where we let her off with the fellows promising her that they'd pick her up at the same location no later than 5 p.m. today. She was to wait for them inside the University's quadrangle in front of the library.

Then, after a somewhat more emotional parting than usual for Eve and me, they drove me off to my four locations for the day. But before I discuss where they were taking me, some explanation might be in order as to why these four places were chosen. The reason for these particular ones was that today's Standard for me was one of the pivotal ones for any world to satisfy completely before a full and successful accreditation could be issued. There must be full compliance with this Standard at the time of our survey. Otherwise, a provisional occupancy may be granted or a cancellation could be issued, which is something we have never had to do. In fact, probation of any kind has been an extremely rare outcome. For at least 95% of these surveys we've been able to issue full accreditation, some even with commendations. And if anyone wanted to stymie this accreditation process, this Standard would be one they would most certainly like to prevent being surveyed or reported on.

In addition to deciding which specific sites I needed to assess, I came to the conclusion that I had to draw a defining line when it came to someone making mistakes that became progressively more harmful and threatening to larger and larger numbers of people. In other words, I needed to determine when certain acts evolved from being a simple mistake that someone apologizes for and subsequently redresses it in some manner. The individual may possibly even perform some necessary penance and resolve not to repeat it again. Next, I had to decide when those simple mistakes morphed into conscious, repetitive decisions and choices that cause greater and greater harm to more and more people and to the world around them.

I've heard Eve describe to others the story about the Four Horsemen of the Apocalypse. In her retelling it, she explained that they represented to her the four worldwide calamities of war, terror, genocide and enslavement. And borrowing this description of hers, I used these four unspeakable tragedies for my survey that day. Using the help of my four companions, I chose to visit various memorials, museums and monuments to see if they have occurred on this world.

These four human tragedies epitomize how simple mistakes, uncorrected and magnified repeatedly over time, become vehicles for an evil that could expose the very darkest aspect of this world's descendents from Eve and I. Frankly, this day could cause me to hang my head in shame, if what we began those eons ago after our leaving Eden, became transformed into such tragedy and loss. But I was determined to stay hopeful, as I began the first tour of the four locations, that this world would get high marks in this Standard come Saturday.

On the way to our first stop, we ducked into another print shop and had another thousand of our questionnaires printed to hand out at each of the survey sites we were to visit. I would not be handing any out this day, nor had I actually done that much prior to this survey. I needed to focus on what I saw, heard and felt. As mentioned before, reviewing the results of these handouts would have to be done by Eve and me on Saturday.

So after some discussion, it was decided that we would begin the day at the site furthest away and end the day closer to Eve, avoiding some backtracking later on. That meant we went first to the Memorial Site where the Twin Towers once stood. It was here that I studied and reflected on the causes, methods and rationale for terrorism. But most of all, I saw the terrible, unspeakable effects of its twisted logic gone absolutely mad. There is no reason or excuse, in the entire Universe, for actions such as this site represented. It was a crime against all life. It represented a negation of it, and those who seek to perpetrate such acts as these are not human. They possess no qualities or sensibilities of any humanity... anywhere. The combination of raw hatred, deluded justification and unexplainable evil represented by these acts of terror made me shudder.

What forces or events had brought individuals to conceive of, plot and carry-out such an unimaginable act? The mistakes that led up to the decisions and choices that culminated in such terror were beyond my ability to grasp. And all this horror was plotted in a part of the world that Eve and I began life. It filled me with such shame and sorrow.

And after an hour of meditation and grappling with the senselessness of what happened there, I eventually left the viewing area overlooking the ongoing construction, and returned to the waiting cab. Today was definitely not going to be one that I will look back on with any pleasure or comfort. I couldn't help but wonder what Eve and I set in motion all those years ago, if this day is going to repeatedly reveal grim reminders of misunderstandings and mistakes being used to justify malignant crimes, like that which I had just witnessed.

Certainly, the next site offered little more comfort. I was driven to Pier 86, at the west end of 46th Street, where the Intrepid Sea-Air-Space Museum was located. It was to provide me with some insight into the next apocalyptic horseman that I was to investigate... war. And in touring this complex of ships and airplanes I was struck by two opposing messages: the horror of war with its maniacal origins framed by the selfless bravery of those who died or were wounded trying to combat it and achieve some measure of peace and good will.

The forces at play here were as defining and contrasting as the colors of black and white, the forces of evil versus goodness or of societies filled with murderous insanity versus those struggling to achieve harmony and ever-lasting peace.

Viewing what was on display here demonstrated the ever-competitive drive to develop more sophisticated equipment and methods to wage war and to defend freedom. But I couldn't help but wonder how far can one country continue to commit so much of its treasure and citizenry in the fight for peace? No one country can expend most if not all its resources to maintain this world's delicate balance. Bankruptcy of spirit and economy will inevitably come to this land unless a change of focus for ALL of this world's inhabitants is made clear and reinforced with absolute authority. Eve and I have some real persuading to do come Sunday; that was becoming only too evident.

And in case you are wondering, there had not been a moment so far this morning that I had had a premonition or sensation that I was being watched or followed. And that continued to be the case right up to the time this particular day came to a frightening conclusion. The exhibits and memorials that I was visiting were too important for me to have any thought about my own personal safety. The sacrifices and tragedies represented in these four places squelched my personal feeling of threat and made me feel very small and unimportant. Hero's don't necessarily have to lose their lives in an act of bravery; they sometimes are more often innocent citizens or unwitting bystanders who are caught up in the hatred and madness of a hideous cause or crime. The millions lost in these conflicts were reverently represented, and their staggering losses were painstakingly recorded in these displays and memorials. Most people don't volunteer for heroic acts. They come in an instant. They snatch you up by the hundreds of thousands, even apparently by the millions. The absolute agony of what I witnessed that day through these exhibits was taking a toll. I was losing focus.

So, trying to regain some composure, I asked Eddie and his three associates, all of whom had been busy handing out the questionnaires while I toured the aircraft carrier and spoke with the men and women in uniform, the various docents and some in the general public, to drive me next to E. 42nd Street. While there, I would visit a Center dedicated to education and training for prevention of intolerance, racism, sexism and the Third Horseman: genocide. Unfortunately, this next, bewildering aberration of human behavior seemed to be endemic... it's almost everywhere and ongoing. And as soon as it occurred, the denials or disregard of its existence begin by those who might have stopped it. It's like society's plate was already full with "The Troubles", and this "problem" was not something that countries want to expend time sorting out or stopping. The list of occurrences seemed endless; examples included Armenia, the Jewish Holocaust, Cambodia, Rwanda, Sudan and using slower and somewhat more subtle methods, women in far too many cultures.

This particular issue was sadly something unique to this world alone. Eve and I had not found it elsewhere. Nowhere else we've traveled and surveyed does the impulse to eliminate entire segments of a society or country exist. And after speaking to a wide variety of individuals there and seeing the Center's exhibits, I left feeling stunned. What is it with this world? It's like a terrifying virus has permeated the planet and has deadly outbreaks on a regular basis. I could only conclude that, with the exception of the good people I had been meeting and reading about through this week's survey, there still existed a cultural blindness that allowed these acts to unfold. Eve and I had to address this.

And finally, sometime around mid-afternoon, I directed Eddie to drive me to the New York Historical Society building, located on Central Park West between 77th and 78th Streets, so I could study a recent exhibit on slavery. Enslavement was to be the Fourth and final Horseman that I would examine in regards to the fourth Standard of mine. Sadly, the host country that Eve and I were camping in had one of the saddest histories of this activity; one that lasted for hundreds of years when it shipped and bought slaves brought over from Africa. But then, I again found that women too often were still being abused and incarcerated in this trade as well.

In fact, to a greater or lesser degree, each of these offenses against humanity, as represented by the Four Horsemen, were ongoing to this day. I left this final exhibit dumbfounded and unfortunately unaware of my surroundings. And I nearly paid dearly for that loss of awareness.

The agreement I had with "The Apples" was that they would go ahead and pick up Eve at Columbia University where she had been investigating her charge for the day, while I finished up at the Historical Society's exhibit and discussed related issues with its staff and any visitors that came in. Axe did stay back with me to hand out the remaining questionnaires to people coming into and going out of the building. But he left ahead of me to hail our cab and have it parked and ready for me, once I left the building. Unfortunately, it took me a little longer than any of us expected due to my becoming engrossed in this exhibit and discussing its ramifications with some visiting dignitaries from similar museums in the States of Virginia and Maryland. The purpose of their respective museums was also to ensure that no one would ever forget this human tragedy.

Knowing that I had held everyone up, I hurriedly left the building and walked as fast as my bandy legs would allow. As previously mentioned, I wobble when I try to walk fast. It always appears like I am an oversized, wounded duck when I do. But I knew everyone was tired and wanted to go home for a well deserved meal and some rest. This had already been a very long week, and it was still not anywhere near over. And I worried that Eve, despite her remarkable resilience, was becoming overtired. So I worried and tried to run.

When I got to the corner of 78th Street and Central Park West, I was relieved to see there was a street light that regulated the flow of speeding traffic. And for some reason, at that moment, I was the only person waiting at the crosswalk, which led almost directly to our parked cab. Everyone in it was waving at me to hurry up. I became confused as I began to cross the street when I noticed that Eddie and Robert, who were standing outside on the passenger side of the cab, yelled something that I couldn't hear; and Eve had rolled down the window by the backseat, driver's side and was also trying to get my attention. I couldn't hear either of them due to the traffic noise and my lousy, progressively failing hearing. In a way it was a blessing up until then, not having to hear the full blast of horns, screeches, brakes and yelling that normally permeated throughout the city.

Anyway, when the light changed and the "Walk" light flashed, I quickly left the corner curb and proceeded to begin following the well-marked crosswalk over to them and better hear what they were shouting. But suddenly, as if it just appeared out of nowhere, a sleek, black vehicle, one with its windows all tinted so no one could see who or what was inside, sped straight at me. And it was frightfully evident it had no intention of stopping. If anything, it was accelerating as it got closer. It was then I realized that was what all the yelling was about from Eve and Robert. They saw it coming long before I did.

And as quickly as I noticed it, not more than three feet from me, and its front bumper aimed right at my chest, Irene unexpectedly appeared but only visible to me, and probably to Eve, at the time. She yanked me backwards onto the sidewalk; suddenly and forcefully enough that the vehicle's outside edge just brushed my shirt tail, which had been pulled free. And as I plopped down, I noticed for the first time that both my sandals were lying on the street. In an instant the onrushing vehicle turned onto 78th Street and vanished as quickly as it appeared. It was senseless to try to follow it or yell at the driver or anyone else who was inside. It and whoever was inside disappeared in the congestion of the late afternoon.

Then just as quickly as she appeared, Irene was gone; but not before she whispered to me, "You must be more careful, Adam! You're in grave danger."

Immediately thereafter, Eve ran up and leaned over me, frantically asking if I was alright. But all this was happening so fast, it wasn't until much later that I remembered Irene's words of caution and told Eve.

Understandably, she and everyone else in the taxi were shaken by this possible, near-fatal accident. But everyone, except Eve, agreed that it was probably just that… a near accident. It wasn't until later when I had enough composure and something to eat and drink that I began to think differently. Irene was right. Something or someone was determined to do me harm. Fortunately, it did not appear to be Eve that was the focus of this plot. But why me?

Just the same, Eddie and Robert insisted that they take us on an indirect route back to our campsite again. And we had instructions to meet them at a different location again the next morning. Anxiety was building in everyone. This narrow escape only added to everyone's feelings of concern; it was now bordering on dread.

ELEVEN: THE EXPLORING/INVENTING STANDARD

I didn't envy Adam, given the day he had ahead. Mine would be centered entirely on the campus of this university. I knew he was going to have to make multiple stops to get the information he needed. Without a doubt, our shifting around the Standards this time, as we always do, left him with all the more complicated ones. But he never complains. I am worried, though. This sudden interest in him by someone is not a good sign. My hope is it's just a stalker or someone who is intrigued with his appearance and overly curious about the locations he goes to. Maybe they are reporters for some news organization. I have to trust that they mean neither of us any harm.

Anyway, after I was left off in front of the 116th Street and Broadway entrance to the University for my second assignment here, I had to review my plans for the day. Briefly, I needed to reconsider the classes I would drop in on, the professors that I would speak with and the library research I would need to do. From the few mental notes I made earlier this morning before Adam and I got up, I broke down the day's investigation of exploration and inventiveness into three investigative categories: the humanities, the other inhabitants of this world besides people and ending with any extraterrestrial pursuits or discoveries that were being documented.

Once I approached the entrance to the University, I was struck again by the towering, ornate buildings around and before me. This place has been the collective seat and origin of so much knowledge for at least two hundred years. Certainly there were older institutions of its caliber scattered around the world, but most likely none that were better. And stored in its libraries and vaults had to be the collective knowledge of what is known about pre and recorded history. Even for me, who had traveled so many thousands of years, to thousands of worlds, this place was quite humbling in its design and purpose. It wasn't forbidding nor was it altogether inviting. It demanded a seriousness of purpose and a dedication to truth. I felt those weren't bad requisites for some of the things that

Adam and I would have to say come Sunday in St. Patrick's Cathedral.

Because of the early hour, before many of the buildings or classes would be opened or started, I decided to begin my survey in the libraries. I sensed one or more of them would be open all the time for students to use, and I was right. The immense Butler Library was open, even though their Spring Break was not far off. And it was here I began my study of the other inhabitants of this world, excluding humanity. I focused on natural history, zoology, botany, paleontology and something called evolution.

Now, don't get me wrong. I full-well realized after examining the countless volumes given up to the study of evolution, that it represents a mostly creditable alternative to what Adam and I have been responsible for starting on this most remarkable world. It's just that we have a different viewpoint. Ours is that humanity began with us. Believe what you will about us; that we are creations of fiction, myth, dreamtime fable or propaganda. Let me say here and now: we are not charlatans or figments of someone's overactive imagination. Neither are we claiming sole responsibility for anything. It's just that where we began our lives on this world, there were no others. And we were given the impression, or more accurately, the blunt ultimatum by our own Creator that we were the first humans. Someone had to be. And apparently it began with us.

I find the linkage between animals and

humanity intriguing and worthy of study and conjecture. But I would also suggest that scholars and students alike keep in mind the more mysterious aspects about life. The unknown and unknowable are possibly even more important to any scientist or in any scientific endeavor. Some explorations do not ever end. The expanse of the Universe should convince everyone of that fact. And the issue of how and when humanity came into being should ever-remain one of those mysteries. It keeps us humble and honest.

Finally, after having finished my study of this first major, exploratory realm, I must congratulate everyone who has spent time, energy and fortune examining the millions of life forms on this world. It is a remarkable achievement. Nowhere else in all the Universe can you find the diversity of life that is found here. Of that you can be more than certain. We know. We've seen them all, and this is the last inhabited world left to survey. My one last observation on this subject, however, would be that as much care as has been spent on exploration, at least as much should have been and needs to be spent on preservation. There appears to be an ever-expanding clumsiness, which is resulting in extinction of species. This is worrisome to me, and it foretells a dangerous trend for the entire planet. Do not let this process become irreversible; and believe me, you will not know exactly when that happens. We've seen that, as well, happen on other worlds.

To complete my review and survey of this

first category, I next went to the Low Memorial Library and took the opportunity to examine of some of their magnificent collections on this subject. By mid-morning I was satisfied that I had studied this aspect of exploration enough.

From there, it was only a short walk away to the Earl Building, where I would begin my survey of the second major category: the study of how humanity has explored itself over thousands of years. Next to the endless task of trying to survive each day, this endeavor of trying to define what it means to be human became the endless preoccupation of each man, woman and child on this planet; and still is to this day. I can see it in the billboards and advertisements that Adam and I pass by each day. It seems to be both a fascination and a lifelong goal: to become acquainted with and possibly to know thyself.

And the earliest beginnings of this process, once our species survival had been at least marginally achieved, were to develop rudimentary rites, rituals and sacrifices. These serious self-explorations soon afterward led to formalizing observances of particular religions. And often, these observances said as much about the peoples who practiced them as they did of their Deity or deities who they worshiped or feared.

Obviously, Adam and I capitalizing on our earliest experiences in and out of The Garden, offered our sons and their families the foundation of a religious faith, but apparently it wasn't long after we departed this world that an infinite variety of them began to arise in pockets everywhere. Everyone seemed to have a different answer to the ultimate "Why?" And the imagination and desire to worship, give thanks and to ask for help and guidance led to countless other ways to worship. The tragedy was that so often conflict arose, often fostered by the zeal of certain members of a faith, sect or nation to convert or dominate people who practiced otherwise.

And to discover how humanity pursued this process, I next went to Earl Hall, just west of the Low Memorial Library. It is the University's center for the study of religion. Soon enough, I had confirmed my suspicions regarding this world's religious quests, and I headed north through the maze of lofty buildings and monuments to Havemeyer Hall, my next stop in the study of humanity.

It was in this building, as in the other four I went to regarding this immense undertaking, that I attended some classes, spoke to professors and students and skimmed through various documents. And it was in this Hall that I examined some of the seminal exploration into the building blocks of life and structures that surround and allow it to exist.

The first discipline was the field of chemistry. Nothing demonstrates better the historical significance and roadmap of the importance of this discipline than the creation and expansion of the Periodic Table of the Elements. If I could have chosen a scientific field in this world to become immersed in, this would have been it. I spent a wondrous hour in there.

Quickly, given the task ahead, I then rushed north again to the Schapiro Center, where the Engineering and Physical Sciences Departments were located. Whether it was the building of the Egyptian Pyramids, the Great Wall of China, the Golden Gate Bridge, the Three Gorges Dam or mapping the Genome, this Center represented an inventive legacy that was breathtaking. There are other planets that easily match the social advancement of this one, but none have the scope of exploration and inventiveness. At that moment, I couldn't help but be proud to have once been a small part of this world.

And the last stop in my quest for understanding humanity's ability to explore itself and its potential was to visit the Fayereather Bulding, which houses the History and Sociology Departments, along with some joint Law School programs. I spent two exhausting hours here, digesting the historical record of humanity's unquenchable thirst for exploring new frontiers, whether geographical or social.

After seeing all this, I had left my third and final category of exploration to survey; the one that extended into extraterrestrial regions. And to finish my day I went to two buildings on each side of the Schapiro Center: Pupin Hall and the Mudd Building. Pupin Hall housed the Physics and Astrophysics Departments, with an astronomical observatory located on the top of the building. And the Mudd Building incorporated the Mathematics,

Computer Science and Applied Physics Departments.

It was in these buildings that I reviewed the rudimentary attempts of humanity to explore the outer reaches of the Universe. Even the earliest peoples began to dabble in geometry and astronomical landmarks to build their monuments and establish order within their cultures. The Sun, Moon, Stars and Planets were integral parts of their daily lives. And it was with these tools that this exploration beyond themselves began. Over the centuries, with more sophisticated optics, more integrated mathematical calculations and genius, the cosmos began to open itself up to humanity. To date, this drive to explore has led to some remarkable advances in a relatively short time span. Rockets and space vehicles are now poised to explore more of the moon and other planets farther away in the Earth's solar system. This world is nudging open a magnificent doorway of exploration. And, increasingly, my hope is that its inhabitants have the time remaining to push it fully open. If they can, what awaits them is breathtaking. Adam and I know.

In summary, then, before Adam and I had our sit-down discussion and prepared any recommendations and a final decision on accreditation this Saturday, I can honestly say that I have been the most impressed at the advances in connection with this Standard. The historical record clearly shows that humanity struggled for centuries to meet its basic bodily needs before developing some rudimentary socialization skills. There then began to follow this remarkable period of inspiration and drive to discover, innovate and explore… themselves, their immediate surroundings and the infinite space beyond this world. There is still a balance yet to be achieved before this world arrives at a mature sense of itself. It has to develop a global self-esteem that does not require or foster threat, bondage or conquest and a maturity that shuns a bullying arrogance. Instead, this renewed self has to be refocused and redirected into an ever-present audacity of discovery, wonder and awe.

That said, without question, even without knowing what Adam has found out with his surveys, this Standard represents this world's most ambitious and successful achievement. My initial impression is that if the same dedication and energy had been equally focused on modifying certain behaviors and appetites, there would be no limit as to how great this world could be. Sadly, the ability to communicate effectively appears to have always lagged in its inventiveness and urge to explore. My impression at this moment is that overall it is still in adolescence as a world. It may have made striking advances in some respects, but it must do better as a people. It must.

By 5 p.m., Eddie's cab, with the two other "Apples", as Adam like to call them all, arrived at the curb on Broadway and 116th Street to pick me up. It was a relief to see them. I was becoming progressively more exhausted with each passing day. I was so grateful tomorrow was to be our last survey… forever. And I knew Adam felt the same way.

Our drive down to pick up Adam at our prearranged spot on Central Park West was blissfully quiet. All the fellows had been working diligently passing out and collecting Adam's questionnaires, and they were also exhausted. They told me the trunk of the cab was filled with boxes of one's already filled out! Saturday was looking like a very full day for all of us.

And as I spied Adam at the corner where we were to pick him up, to my surprise, as he began crossing the street to where we were idling, Eddie suddenly yelled out, "LOOK OUT, ADAM!! THERE'S A CAR COMING RIGHT AT YOU…!!!"

But the horror of this scene to me was that it was too late for him to dodge it. I knew, without any doubt, he was going to be struck by that fast-moving vehicle. There was no way he, at his age, had anywhere near the agility to fling himself backward out of its oncoming path. And there was no question in my mind that it was aiming straight for him. This was no random accident unfolding. Adam was in mortal danger.

Then I screamed, as I lunged out of the taxi window, "STOP!! GO BACK, ADAM!! FOR GOD'S SAKE… GO BACK!!!"

But just then, only recognized by me, because of her unique quality to only appear to the individual or individuals that were meant to see her, Irene suddenly appeared and grabbed Adam by the waist and yanked him backwards, allowing the speeding black sedan or truck to rush past him, just grazing his shirttail. Apparently, she yanked him so hard that his sandals were left in place on the pavement, and the skidding car ran over them, as it turned the corner and disappeared from sight.

Rushing over, in between the cars that were now slowing down and stopping, I nodded to Irene that I was able to manage from this point on. I leaned over Adam who had now raised up to sit on the curb. "ARE YOU OK!?" I breathlessly asked, knowing full well that he wasn't.

"Yep," he replied, in his usual denial of most reality swirling around him. "But that was just about as close a call as I need for one day. Did you see who did that? Do you have any kind of a description of who it might have been?"

"No, I'm sure we don't," I replied. "It all happened so fast; there was no time to do anything but react to your vulnerable and exposed circumstance. They got away. But it is certain that they meant to do you harm. Someone wants to stop what you or we are doing. For the first time in our lives, at least one of us is at great risk. There is great danger present all around us, Adam. And I am afraid for you."

FRIDAY

TWELVE: THE LOVING STANDARD

Everything happened so fast when that car, or whatever it was, zoomed past me that I have little memory of it all. One thing is for sure: ole Irene knows how to yank a fellow backwards when she wants to. My back is still sore from her doing that! But what if she hadn't? It doesn't bear thinking about.

And then there was Eve. She was more upset than I've ever seen her! You'd think the person driving that black thing was trying to kill me, which she is convinced that whoever was driving it… was. And I suppose she might be right. But it just doesn't fit. Why me? Why now? I guess if anything, I'm relieved it wasn't Eve that was the focus of someone's anger. And it's for sure; we'll now have to take some extra precautions.

And we did. It started from the moment that Eve and "the Apples" got me back into their taxi cab. Eddie then drove us back and forth, in and around and up and down mid and upper Manhattan. He figured no one would try to follow us through some of the more congested streets in upper Harlem. Plus, he made a telephone call to a couple of his pals to watch out for us and for anyone looking suspicious who might be following. If they did see someone like that, they were to block them off and try to get their identities. It was clear this episode had scared everyone, and they were on high alert.

Eventually, as darkness enveloped the city, we were let off a few blocks from our campsite, at Eve's and my insistence. Our being driven around for over two hours had lessened our anxiety, and once we got settled down, we gave each other our daily report. It was evident that we were still nervous about what the next day might bring, but we had no choice. This was our final assignment. It had to be completed. Not to finish it meant almost certain cancellation of this world's accreditation. And that was the last thing that we wanted to happen. It was like our firstborn. It was the closest thing that Eve and I ever had to a home. Although most of our memories had long ago faded as to what all actually happened here, our emotional attachment to this world was by far the strongest of anywhere we had previously visited. We were determined to see this through.

And luckily both of us were going to be in only one location for our final survey. There would be no more of this dashing about, whether on a college campus or through the streets of the city. Eve would be safely sheltered within the United Nations complex, and I would have the added protection of all "the Apples" tomorrow, as I canvassed Central Park for my last survey. I felt I'd be secure with them looking out for me.

And by 11 p.m. we finally fell asleep, relieved tomorrow would be our final survey... ever.

Not wanting to be separated from Eve when out in the public, I rode over with our crew early the next morning to the United Nations Building complex and let Eve off. Because of a general consensus that all "the Apples" should be with me that day as we strolled through Central Park, I instructed Irene to accompany Eve, in case anything should occur that might require her protection. Irene argued a bit with me, but I insisted. I couldn't leave Eve otherwise. Eve, of course, never knew that I had done this. I couldn't bear anything happening to her, and this was the least I could do. And I firmly believed that she, along with Irene, could face this world's entire range of threats and still overcome whatever happened. Together, they are a mighty force. So, with a kiss and a follow-up wave, we drove off so I could tackle my last day's assignment.

And to do so, I instructed Eddie to drive back to Central Park West and 106th Street and drop us off. He was then to drive the cab down to 65th Street and park somewhere in that area for the day. Once he had done that, he was to ride the #10 Manhattan Bus back up to 106th Street and meet us somewhere around the Great Hill, located with the Park. *(see Appendix for "Runner's Map" of Central Park, both the "Intact" and "Exploded Views")* But before we divided up, we stopped by our usual print shop and picked up another batch of questionnaires for everyone to hand out throughout the day.

After we reassembled on a walking path fronting onto 106th Street, I outlined what our party was to do that day. I had been giving considerable thought to it before getting up that morning. Three distinct tasks needed to be completed before the day was over. First, as previously alluded to, I needed to have them hand out our leaflets to anyone and everyone we could throughout the day. They were to show no preference as to who should get one. All one thousand had to be distributed by 5 p.m. Next, I needed to spend time with a variety of individuals and couples, having honest and confidential discussions with them. To do so, I needed to do whatever I could to put them at ease and allow them to give me their undivided attention. And finally, and most importantly, I needed to personally select individuals and couples from five different areas in the Park to reassemble into five groups, representing the five areas that I chose them from.

They were all to meet at 3 p.m. in the Sheep Meadow, just west of the Park's Mall. And between the times I made this non-negotiable request and they met, I would give each individual or couple a list of five questions that they were to discuss in these five groups. Each group would eventually give their summation back to me by 5 p.m. "The Apples" and I needed to pick Eve up immediately after that.

The five questions that I wanted the five groups to assemble and discuss were: What is love? What does it mean to be loved? What does it mean to love someone? What are the obstacles to loving? And how or why does loving someone cease?

There would be only one summation from each of the five groups. And I would impress on each person how significant this assignment was. To some degree, the very continued existence of this world's human endeavors might depend upon their honesty and thoughtfulness. Little did any of them know when they got out of bed this morning that such a heavy of burden would befall them. Maybe that's a lesson for everyone. Treat each day as if whatever decision you make will impact the quality and quantity of all life around you. Certainly, it's beginning to appear to me that by the end of this week some such message will be necessary for the citizens of this world. Having hope is one vital key to achieving lasting peace and complete harmony, but it is not enough. People must act on that hope. Each person must begin acting like life itself depends on their every thought, decision and spoken word. Far too much has been taken for granted, far too long. That's becoming too evident to me.

I'm not sure whether it will be Eve or I who will be speaking on Sunday. We usually decide who that will be by the end of our review on Saturday. Certainly, if I were the one selected, I would waste no time mincing words. This world is in trouble.

So, finally, armed with our questionnaires and instructions, we began our survey of my very last Standard at 8 a.m. sharp. But at no time during the day did everyone of "The Apples" leave me alone. There were always two of the fellows either beside, in front or behind me. They tried to be somewhat inconspicuous, so as not to alarm anyone. But they took their bodyguard duties very seriously, as did I.

Taking a deep breath as we were about to begin the survey of this last Standard, I turned to my cohorts and simply said, "Let's finish what we've all started together, what do you say?"

Everyone nodded in agreement, and we began the next seven hours canvassing as many people as we could with the same five questions that were to be discussed in the large groups.

During that time, to allow me to get the most honest and forthright answers, I walked dogs; pushed baby strollers; shagged baseballs; held one end of jump ropes; fixed roller skate laces; helped launch model boats, planes, cars and trucks; asked joggers and bicyclists to spare me a moment or two; strolled with the less agile; lunched with groups of foreign exchange students and sun-bathed with office workers from various nearby museums.

Their answers to my questions ran the full spectrum of the deepest human emotional need: to be loved and to love. Many immediately quoted religious scripture, defining love by beginning with words like "love is…….". Others were more pensive, as if searching their own experiences to carefully craft something deeply prized or sadly lost. Everyone framed their answers in the present, past or future tense; some as if they were waiting expectantly for something wondrous to happen to them. They used terms like "loving" or "unloving", "loved" or "unloved" and "lovable" or "unlovable".

Always there was a specific party involved, whether it was just between themselves and a partner, a family member, dear friend or neighbor, community, region, nation or even the world.

And running throughout almost everyone's responses, there seemed to be an element of disappointment or longing. Some had experienced or were experiencing the bliss and indescribable peace of being or feeling truly loved, whether by another person or through faith in a treasured covenant with their God or both, but far too many were searching and hoping. And some it appeared had given up any hope of something this precious entering their lives. They were convinced they had become unlovable.

Overall, by 3 p.m., I had the impression that the vast majority of people I spoke with had been honest and sincere. It was almost as if they were relieved to have a chance to voice something that was so deeply felt, rarely experienced but desperately desired. And the conclusions reached by the five discussion groups paralleled the responses I got from my individual encounters.

Throughout those seven hours "the Apples" and I made our way initially from the area around the Great Hill, to the North Meadow Ball Fields, around the Reservoir, to The Great Oval and The Lake area and finally to the Carousel grounds. By the time we had completed that circuit, all the questionnaires had been passed out and that left me able to lead our crew, intact, back to the Sheep Meadow where the five groups were to meet.

I had my four companions each sit in four of the groups, and I took the fifth. They were instructed not to facilitate any discussion, but let the individual group find its way. They were just supposed to gather the final statements from each one and deliver them to me. Eve and I would study them the next day.

But even before Eve and I were to review them, I had a good idea what they would say. I sensed they would confirm what I had heard repeatedly all day. I almost felt like I had been inside a confessional the entire day, listening to the longings and admissions of so many people. And to summarize, what follows is a portion of what I heard. It was the deepest of human emotions, often simply expressed in single words and occasionally in short phrases. I never doubted the truth of what I was told or read. Here is your world's summation of life's most precious gift to one another.

1. What is love? Respect, sharing, caring, forgiving, compromising, loyalty, compassion, serenity, fairness, openness, maturity, honesty, kindness, humility, endurance, acceptance, unfailing, understanding, knowing, trusting, brimming with hope now and for the future, ability to freely communicate fears, feelings, hopes, failures and ultimately that it is the greatest gift anyone can give or receive.

2. What does it mean to be loved? Finding shelter in a confusing or hopeless situation, not being alone, being accepted for who you are or will become and knowing all the endless gifts listed in question number one above are yours to receive.

3. What does it mean to love someone? Being able to give without reservation or regard to consequences, being fully and completely committed to him, her, it or them and having peace that surpasses all probability or understanding.

4. What are the obstacles to loving? Selfishness, meanness, bullying, domineering, indifference, demanding; an obsession to be respected when that only comes from casting aside one's own personal importance.

5.   How does loving someone cease? Abuse, betrayal, a widening gulf of differences or indifference accompanied by there not being enough caring to share or compromise, a change in outlook or goals accompanied by a lack of any desire or ability to adapt, understand or nurture and an immature outlook or expectation without the commitment to do all that number one above entails.

Then, suddenly, I realized that it was almost 5 p.m. and that the United Nations Building would be closing most of its offices soon; and I didn't want Eve to be standing unprotected outside on some street corner. I yelled out to Eddie to run over and get his cab and drive through on 66th Street and meet us here at the Sheep Meadow's road edge. We could then quickly head over to Roosevelt Drive and hurry down to meet Eve. But I knew that there was no time to waste. Something inside me signaled danger was at hand. Our only safety was to be together and then to face it. And as Eddie jogged off, I screamed, uncharacteristically, "HURRY UP, EDDIE! RUN, MAN! ... RUN!!

Once Eddie loaded the four of us into the cab, we only took ten minutes to get to the front entrance of the U.N. Building.   And luckily, we were just in time to see that Eve was beginning to walk out the front gate onto the sidewalk. Breaking all the traffic rules so rigidly enforced in the city, Eddie wheeled us around and pulled squarely in front of Eve, and I threw open the door to let her in. And with a great sigh of relief, I called out, "Hurry,

Eve, get in!"

"What's wrong?" she asked surprised, as she climbed in beside me.

"I have been having a horrible feeling something bad was going to happen to us. So, I had Eddie hurry to get here. I'm so relieved to see you and that you are unharmed!"

And as we pulled away from the curbside, we heard sounds of wheels squealing and the first gunshots. Spinning around, Robert, who was in the back seat with Eve and I, glanced out the rear window and saw two figures about 100 feet away running towards us. They were exchanging fire with two guards stationed at the southern perimeter of the security fence surrounding the front of the U.N. Building, as they tried to make their way toward us. It was clear even at that distance that we were their intended targets.

"Get us out of here!!" Robert yelled to Eddie, just as I was pulling Eve fully into the back seat. There wasn't even time to close the back door. Just as Eve's trailing foot cleared the running board, the lunging of the cab slammed it shut.

"What's happening?!!" Eve screamed at me, barely above the din of screeching tires, shouts and shots being fired at us and at our assailants.

"We're under attack!!" I yelled back. "Someone is trying to kill me or us. You must duck down as low as you can!... RIGHT NOW!!!"

Luckily, we had already arranged that J.L. and Axe ride up front with Eddie; that left Robert the only other passenger in the rear seat with us.

And as soon as Eddie accelerated away from the curb, he began the most remarkable feat of weaving his way through the five o'clock rush hour, New York City traffic, all of it seemingly heading in the same direction as we were... off the island of Manhattan.

No sooner had we pulled into the flow of traffic than he was turned eastward onto FDR Drive and heading south. With his horn blaring the entire time, he weaved in and out of traffic often using the shoulder of the road to pass slowed or stopped traffic. And at the same time, once we got on this main artery, Robert noticed that a black vehicle, similar to if not the same one which tried to run me down the day before, took up the chase. And it seemed to Robert that driver made no effort to dodge or to avoid side-swiping any car or truck that was in his way. The intent was clear. Nothing was going to stop this attack until it was successful.

After we got onto FDR Drive, Robert frantically called out to me, "Take off those blasted sandals and put on this pair of gym shoes that we always keep on hand for any pick-up ballgame. Also, put on this overcoat. We've got to cover up your tourist costume. Your show is over and done. Now it's our turn to call the shots. And Eve, here's another coat for you to put on. Axe! Give Eve your cap, and I'll give Adam mine. Pull them well down over your ears, tucking any loose hair up underneath. Who knows? We may have to jump out of here unexpectedly, at anytime. You're both going to have to blend unnoticed into a crowd. That will be your only protection; if you have to leave us."

Once Eddie had driven about ten minutes, he made a right hand turn onto E. Houston Street, then south onto Clinton; and finally he merged us into the traffic on Delancy Street. It led us across the Williamsburg Bridge into Brooklyn. But just as we thought we had lost the first vehicle chasing us, there was another one that apparently had been positioned ahead of time to take up the chase if need be; as were others we were soon to learn. It was uncanny how they appeared whenever we happened to pull well ahead of one or move suddenly into another busy corridor.

This meant that Eddie had to keep squeezing his way in and around buses, cars, truck, trailers, anything and everything on the busy roadways. And by now we, too, were striking vehicles around us. The noise of his honking, yelling, crashing into cars was chilling. Nothing like this had ever happened to Eve and I, and we were petrified.

In the midst of all this happening, Robert had also gotten two blankets that they kept in the back seat to cover us in the evening when it got cooler, and he stuffed them up against the cab's back window.

"We need to try and prevent shattered glass from spraying us, if and when they get any lucky shots off that might strike us," he explained. "In the meantime keep your heads down."

And by the time we were crossing the Bridge, shots were fired directly at us for the first time. Two came through the back window, just as Robert had predicted that they might. Whatever hopes of escape any of us may have had by that time, had now been dashed. We were all targets.

From the Bridge, Eddie entered the Brooklyn-Queens Expressway and then was able to make an impossible maneuver across four lanes of traffic onto the exit to McGuiness Blvd. At that point we lost the second vehicle. But no sooner had we lost it than another one began the chase once we turned onto the Long Island Expressway and entered onto the roadway heading back into Manhattan. Our pursuers seemed to be able to anticipate our every turn. And all the while they twisted, weaved and slammed into other cars; the yelling inside our cab by all of us continued nonstop. None of us were sure, by that point, whether we were going to be able to outrun or outmaneuver these people, whoever they were. They seemed to have eyes everywhere.

Soon after entering the Long Island Expressway, we came to the Queens-Midtown Tunnel and began our weaving through lanes of traffic inside it. The noise only magnified tenfold inside that place. It was horrific. And I felt Eve shaking uncontrollably by that time. I worried that she was becoming paralyzed with fear, and why wouldn't she? I was sick at my stomach. All this work. All this time together. And now we were facing a force determined to stop whatever we were doing or whatever we might say on Sunday. Who could it be?

My random thoughts were interrupted by J.L. calling out, "I think they must have a helicopter overhead, spotting for them. How else can they have all these cars picking up our route? They must all be communicating with one another."

Just then we exited the tunnel and Eddie turned southward onto Third Avenue and then west on 33rd Street. As he twisted his cab through now, very familiar territory, he shouted out, "We are all going to have to bail out of here!! There is no way I can evade them any longer. I want you, Adam and Eve, to exit first; once I pull up to the 8th Street entrance into Penn Station. Robert will give you a couple of subway tokens and you run as fast as you can into the Station and look for the signs directing you to Trains 'A', 'C' or 'E'. Board one as quickly as possible. Once inside, look as inconspicuous and casual as you can. (*see Appendix "Manhattan Subway Map"*).

"Grab a newspaper, if possible, and put it in front of you. Squeeze onto the first car you can get into. You want the train that heads north to Columbus Circle. And it's there you'll get off and find subway train number '1'. It will take you further north. But again you need to get off at the 96th Street Station and go to the platform for trains '2' or '3'. And after you are on board that train, you are to finally exit at the 110th Street Station at Central Park North. You must not under any circumstances go back to your usual campsite. Find a secluded spot not too far from that last subway station and cover yourselves up. Take the blankets that Robert put in the windows. Just shake the glass out of them once you get on the sidewalk. But, you must hurry!! You have no time to waste getting inside Penn Station and blending into the crowd.

"In the meantime, I'm going to dump this heap of a cab; and we'll split up and make our way through the night back to Harlem. We will meet you tomorrow morning at 6 a.m. Be sitting on a park bench on the sidewalk leading north from the Great Hill. There is only one pathway that leads in that direction. Avoid talking to anyone or letting anyone see you once you slip into Central Park. We'll take you to a secure location tomorrow morning. You're no longer safe anywhere. And that's the sad truth."

And before Eve or I could object, he had quickly pulled up to a curbside transfer zone for cabs and buses, and Robert was pushing us out. "Good luck!" he cried out as he handed us the blankets, slammed the rear door and the cab pulled away.

Quickly shaking out the two blankets as we ran into a Penn Station front door, I only had time enough to look over at Eve and mumble, "I'm so sorry this is happening..." but just as soon as I spoke, I was interrupted with a helicopter flying overhead, obviously trying to pinpoint where we were. We both sensed it wouldn't be long before these blood-hounds would be on our trail, if we didn't get out of sight quickly and blend into the mass of commuters underground.

Fortunately, Eve was quick and alert

enough, despite her being so frightened in the cab, to point out the directions we had to go to enter the right corridors, stairways, escalators and ramps. Her doing so allowed us to maneuver remarkably smoothly through those three subway stations. However, because of all the running and commotion that normally takes place during this time, we were never sure whether our determined killers were on our trail or not. But somehow we were able to finally exit at the 110th Street Station and find a densely covered area to hide in overnight.

We were too exhausted to say anything to one another once we laid down, using the blankets Robert gave us and picking up some newspaper along the way to cover over us and some black plastic to cover the ground to protect us from the cold and damp overnight. We didn't review what we saw or learned from our surveys that day. We just collapsed into each other's arms, pulled the two blankets over us and tried to imagine that what we had just experienced never occurred. But sadly, it wasn't over.

THIRTEEN: THE GOVERNING STANDARD

It pained me to see Adam drive off. More than anything, I just wanted to be with him for those last few days. An almost immeasurable length of time had not made our partnership more testy or routine. His gradual and progressive failings and missteps only made him more precious to me. We had no need to hide or protect each other from our limitations or shortcomings. If anything, by now they served to bring us closer together. His fumbling manner and halting speech gave a sincerity and honesty to all he said and did. And most importantly, I knew he loved me far beyond anyone's ability to attach some unit of measure to it. It was limitless and timeless.

As I turned from the street, having comforted myself somewhat with these thoughts, I reviewed in my mind how I needed to approach this, my last survey... ever. I needed it to be thorough. My impression overall, thus far, was that this world needed high marks in this Standard, as well as in the Exploring/Inventiveness one that I had just completed. Much hung in the balance for this planet at this point.

So I decided to divide the day up into two parts. In the morning I would inspect and interview employees and department chiefs within the major satellite sections of the United Nations. They would include UNESCO, UNICEF and the Secretariat. In the afternoon, I would then sit in on any business being conducted by the Security Council or within the General Assembly, along with speaking to as many ambassadors as possible from the various nations.

I wouldn't need a lot of time to spend with each party or official. My focus now would be almost surgical. Adam and I had seen countless worlds grapple with how to best govern themselves and then how to unify themselves to build lasting harmony, peace and prosperity for ALL its citizens. And frankly, from what I had been observing all week thus far, this day was not likely to provide me with a sense of that same outcome.

To begin the morning and throughout the rest of the day, I divided my investigative process into three categories: governance, government and self-rule. And within each of these categories, I had developed over time some assumptions that best assured how a given world would meet this Standard.

And to my pleasant surprise, I had seen that our host country had instituted the three major components of responsible governance: an executive, legislative and judicial branch. And that there had been moderately successful efforts to balance the power associated with each of these over the last 200 or so years. All three categories, here as elsewhere, were founded on a most noble principle of public service and a dedication to the common good. Without this being the case, the accumulation of power inevitably becomes centralized, leading to abuse and tragedy for the governed. Citizens of any locale, nation or an entire world have to acknowledge, recruit and vote into office the best amongst themselves to fill these branches of government.

In addition, for governance to meet the needs of its citizenry, three groups of services must be provided: the enactment and interpretation of laws; the insurance of stability and health by providing competent governmental, medical and social services; and the protection of the population through the use of properly trained police, fire and military personnel; with each of these under civilian direction. It is a testament to the quality of individuals providing all these services when a society is just, peaceful and prosperous.

The second major category I investigate when surveying this Standard is the government structure itself. Here, the primary issues involve how it was established and maintained; coupled with how it decides issues regarding the future welfare of its citizens. Two guiding principles stand out in my experience for there to be a successful and tolerant entity: the overall character of the people within a given society and the balance that is achieved between tradition, precedent and history and that of the inevitable flow of new ideas and changing conditions. A society, like individuals, will develop habits and customs that more and more will define their character and the type of government that will evolve. Only by keeping one eye on the past and the other on the present conditions facing them, can any society insure a stable and progressively humane government. We are what we eat. And most certainly we are what we do and think. The collective habits of any country or world will readily define its character and, most likely, its destiny.

And finally, there is the third category to be investigated; that of self-rule. This is the most fundamental one of the three. Any and every society has to be based on this principle. But it requires two essential components to be successful: an enlightened and involved population, which is nurtured on the democratic principles of a free press, open elections and the secret ballot; and a leadership that is sane, fair and just. If either of these is lacking or abused, self-rule will not evolve nor be successful. Adam and I have seen endless examples of this on a local and regional basis. And happily, we have always seen these two components unite on a worldly basis elsewhere. My question now is whether that has occurred on this world?

These is one final caveat on the subject of self-rule. It cannot become either isolationist or expansionist. Once it is established, each local community, state or nation must decide to bring its uniqueness to the table of humanity; to a place such as I see here at the United Nations. The experience, talents and insight of every self-ruled entity must be shared with others for any world to find a lasting peace and the equitable prosperity for all.

To those who distort or deny these basic tenants of governing, whether by the formation of a meritocracy, theocracy or "terrorocracy", based on privilege, wealth, religion or terror, there will be never-ending harm and deprivation to most inhabitants in such a world. This has been well documented by us in some places we've surveyed before this one, and where it became necessary for these same worlds to alter their basic principles of governmental foundation.

Disturbingly, one subject that Adam and I have already been discussing since our arrival here is the stunning discovery we've made that the part of this world where we first began our family and where it ultimately led to the branching of all civilization has not yet developed even the remotest semblance of an orderly and just society. Most nations in that region, which surround our place of origin, are still battling forces of disruption, arrogance of power, inequity of wealth and indescribable terror. And, as a woman, I am appalled at the abuse of my sisters there and elsewhere. This area is the source of so much trouble throughout this world. Why is that? Honestly, it has given Adam and me the deepest sense of failure; that somehow we were unable to pass on the basic principles of civilized behavior.

The suffering and death brought about by the selfishness and twisted ambitions, theories and beliefs in this region is unmatched... anywhere!

Fortunately, however, the day passed quickly. I was extremely anxious to know how Adam was doing. My having Irene alongside did give me the needed confidence to face the day with minimal thoughts for my own safety. But I worried constantly about Adam's. It never crossed my mind to bring Irene into any conversation or situation... at least not until my very last interview for the day.

I had purposefully saved this encounter for my last one. It was planned that way primarily for sentimental reasons and from a deep-seated urge to explore something that I have just alluded to. It was with the Iraqi Ambassador to the United Nations; the individual who represents the nation that arose around the confluence of two rivers, the Tigris and Euphrates, where our Eden was located.

The interview itself went along the usual lines that the others had throughout the day. By then, I had gathered all the material that I needed for our upcoming summation. And the Ambassador was polite, though somewhat skeptical about my reason for being there. He assumed that my questions involved some bureaucratic investigation or evaluation. However, he did appear somewhat caught off guard when I mentioned to him that I would like him and his family to attend the convocation at St. Patrick's Cathedral in two days for the final report on my findings. Actually, my making that request confounded him.

And it was at that point that all his briskness, along with a congenial insincerity vanished. Pressing on, I began my concluding remarks for this interview by telling him who I actually was and that Adam was accompanying me on this accreditation survey. After hearing this, he made an attempt to rise from his armchair, safely positioned behind a magnificent onyx-appearing desk, and I was sure that he was about to order me out of his office suite.

Sensing this, at that very moment, I quietly asked Irene to appear beside me. Unlike Adam, it was necessary for me to verbally request her appearance. I couldn't just gesture like he does to make this happen. But immediately she did come into full view; resplendent in her shimmering white, flowing gown, tailored as it was to allow her wings to be fully outstretched when the occasion called for it. And she must have decided this was one time when it was. I admit, even I was impressed with her grand appearance.

And the Ambassador heaved back into his armchair, exclaiming, "My God! Who is that?!! Who really are you?!!!"

Patiently, I again very briefly explained who I was and for punctuation asked Irene to produce some evidence of her bona fides and display something of her remarkable abilities. And to my absolute surprise and wonderment, she immediately brought forth an apple. THE APPLE! The one with the large, Adam-originated bite out of it. It was the very same one Adam had bitten into and then set into motion such a wave of events ever-after. At that point both the Diplomat and I were speechless.

Gathering some composure, I concluded the interview with a final message to him. It basically was that he and his government must begin to work even harder to bring peace and stability to his region of the world. I emphasized that time was running out. Patience regarding this world was at a critically low level by now with the very Highest Authority. Too many chances for peace and reconciliation had been squandered or wasted over the eons. The birthplace of civilization must now lead and inspire. And finally, I emphasized that he should make every effort to attend the service at St. Patrick's to get a complete picture of why I was demanding this of him.

And as an aside, I left his office without his uttering another word in reply; he just sat slumped in stunned silence. But I did see him on Sunday, along with who I assumed was his family. They were sitting in the second row of pews. He appeared transfixed throughout my presentation.

It was just after that final reminder to him when I glanced over and saw his desk clock, as it gently chimed, indicating that it was 5 p.m., I realized I was late. It immediately unnerved me to think that Adam might be worriedly waiting on the street for me. Bidding the stone-faced Ambassador farewell, I frantically wove my way down the corridors, stairs and elevators down to the First Street exit. And by the time I hurried outside, I saw Eddie's cab was pulling up to the curb. Adding to my shock and amazement, I then saw Adam fling open the taxi cab's rear door and grab me just as I reached curbside. He briskly pulled me inside it, and to my horror, there was panic in his every move, gesture and command.

From that moment, all my life's assumptions and ever-rosy outlook began changing forever. I fully realized that someone was definitely trying to kill one or all of us. And the noise outside the cab was terrifying; the gunshots, the yelling, screeching of brakes and tires, honking of horns, scraping and crashing sounds, twisting and turning from street to street; and all this time with Adam shielding me as he crouched over me with both of us bent over between the front and back seats.

After what seemed like hours of nerve-wracking noise and confusion, Robert demanded that we change into the overcoats and prepare to exit the cab at Penn Station. Exiting into the streaming mass of people at the Station, along with the panic gripping everyone in the cab, including Adam, was enough to make me want to start screaming. It was at that point I had my first profound premonition that something terrible was going to occur before this final survey had concluded. There was no way this venture was going to end peacefully. But how could that surprise me? What issues and findings had we been uncovering all this last week? It seemed logical something unspeakable would occur before we departed. Desperately, I felt that somehow I had to protect Adam; I sensed that he was the actual target of all this mayhem and threat.

Immediately, after leaving "The Apples", Adam and I did as we were instructed, dashing from platform to platform, transferring trains, making ourselves blend into the throngs as best we could. We never knew who might be following or watching us. We just kept on running until we reached the 110th Street Station at Central Park North. And without a word between us, we hurriedly disappeared in the growing darkness into a dense patch of woods. Our little haven we'd used the previous nights was now off-limits. We knew it had to have been discovered by now.

Adam, bless his heart, gathered up some plastic and scattered cardboard and made us as comfortable a bed as possible. Exhausted, we embraced each other, pulling the two blankets around, while leaving our overcoats on. We gently kissed each other and tried to leave the terrible events of the day behind, as we struggled to escape into a dreamless sleep.

SATURDAY

FOURTEEN: SUMMATION DAY

Adam and I awoke the next morning before daylight. To be honest, I doubt seriously either of us slept more than an hour all night. We were both very scared. Nothing like what happened yesterday had even remotely occurred before... for either of us. And we knew that there was no indication of this ongoing attack having ended. We had simply temporarily escaped their trap the day before. One or both of us was in mortal danger, as were "The Apples", our faithful guardians.

I spoke first. "Do you think we should try to make our way in the darkness over to the Great Hill before daylight? And are you hungry? I know I am. It's been over a day since either of us has had anything to eat, unless you got something yesterday while traversing the Park."

"No, I didn't," Adam answered; his voice sounding raspy and aged, more so than I had ever heard before. "I think our flight to escape yesterday took something out of me. I can hardly lift my head up this morning, I feel so weak."

"I know what you mean," I answered.

"We've got to get some food and liquid in us right away. As soon as our companions meet us, we'll have to ask them to find us some nourishment. We can't go on like we have the last day or so. These surveys were not meant to involve deadly chases or become daily flights for safety and survival. We're exhausted, and yet we still have so much work to do before we are finished here."

"Do you think they could find us a safe place to get more rest and some food?" He plaintively cried. "Otherwise, I'm not going to be much good to you; I can tell."

"Then let's make our way over right away and wait for whoever shows up to help us," I offered.

Our passage over to the Great Hill was stealthy, to say the least. It was like we hop-scotched from behind one tree trunk to the next. If our situation hadn't been so serious, I would have laughed at our appearing to be like some staged, mystery theater performance. But it wasn't. And both of us were still very frightened.

Finally, we arrived in the vicinity of our rendezvous point. For the sake of our not appearing so obvious, Adam suggested that we split up and find a secluded area around the only pathway heading north from the Great Hill towards Harlem. And as dawn was breaking, we each found a spot on opposite sides of the path. Joggers and walkers by now were beginning to start their morning rounds and that added to my uneasiness. Which one of those folks, disguised as early morning exercise enthusiasts, might really be canvassing the area to locate us?

My nervousness steadily increased, until I was jolted further by Axe coming up quietly behind me and whispering, "Eve, it's me, Axe. Are you and Adam ok? We've worried all night about the two of you."

"AXE!" I moaned out loud. "You really startled me!!" I almost hissed, turning to face him in the clear light of early morning. "Forgive my outburst… Honestly, I'm very relieved to see a friendly face. Who's with you?"

"Robert is over on the other side of the path. He will be taking Adam with him to your safe house. But each of us has to split up and take different routes to get there. You and I are going together; when you are ready. In addition, we've arranged for each of you to have something to drink and eat once we arrive at that location."

"Oh, thank you! We need nourishment and hydrating right away! But what about Adam's questionnaires?" I asked. "How are we going to be able to examine those when they are left here in the Park?"

"They're not," he answered. "All throughout the night the four of us went back and forth from their location behind the Conservatory Garden and took them box by box to the safe house. They are all waiting for you there. But it took us all night to do so, once the four of us met again after leaving the cab at Penn Station."

"What eventually happened to Eddie's cab?"

I worriedly asked.

"It was pretty much demolished in that chase yesterday. It's now a total loss."

"Oh, what a terrible shame! And what a mess this has all become! We had no idea that this week would turn out this way; otherwise we would never have accepted the most generous and wonderful help you four have given us. I feel so guilty knowing you've put yourselves in such danger, and now Eddie has lost his means of earning a living. Somehow, Adam and I will make all this up to you. But right now, I just don't know what to say. I'm so sorry."

"We know that, Ms. Eve," Axe replied. "We know. It's been a real honor for us to work with you two. Hell... I mean, 'heck', we probably would have just been hustling or doing something else no count, if you two hadn't come along. But we need to get going now. To delay much longer will put both of us in greater danger. Just follow me."

From that point on we began a maddening process of averting, detouring, skirting, running, climbing and descending front steps, outside doors, down fire escapes, around alleyways and across empty lots of broken bits of whatever trash this or past centuries discarded so carelessly. And all the while, I never saw Adam again until we finally reached our destination.

We must have gone at least ten or eleven blocks northward from Central Park, but it was impossible for me to really know, with all the twists and turns that we were taking. We went in and out of people's apartments; ones occupied by families who apparently Axe and Robert knew and had prepared in advance for our racing through. There were never any exclamations or shouts as we entered their homes. Axe never knocked. The doors were always unlocked and the windows of escape already opened; the pathway was prepared for our flight, wherever we went. It was a well coordinated and executed escape.

But about three quarters of the way through our dashing apartment to apartment, as I gasped for each breath, I had to tell Axe that I was too exhausted to go any further. And I could only imagine how miserable Adam must have been. He appeared much wearier than I did before we began this weaving place to place, after leaving the Park.

Reluctantly, Axe acknowledged my need and broke with the plan of escape by leaving me in a vacant doorway, with my back turned to the street. He then ran down to a nearby telephone booth, one of the few that I ever saw in the neighborhood, and made a quick call to someone. I assumed it was an individual whose home we would eventually be passing through along the way.

When he got back to me, I asked him why he didn't have one of those portable telephones that Adam and I saw everyone using, everywhere. He simply replied, "Can't afford one..." To me, that was a definite sign of this individual's honesty and economic status. He was at the very bottom of the financial food chain. He was a discard. Cunning, stealth, being connected, plunder, embezzlement, scheming, illicit trade, open criminal activity… these were too often the pathways to the financial high ground. Being poor, a minority, and heart-breakingly honest did not allow too many to climb the ladder of opportunity. Too often, these individuals like Axe became stuck and forgotten. And their lives became frozen.

What amazed me about "The Apples", who Adam had miraculously found, was their selfless giving, despite their place in this society. What they had was far more valuable than what was hoarded away in private vaults. They had a seemingly endless supply of hope and perseverance. So Axe couldn't afford a natty little telephone, with all its wondrous abilities. He improvised. He found a way to help me without it.

Running back to me, he announced quietly, "I've arranged for you to have a snack and some fruit juice at the next home we pass through. But we still must hurry. We have to meet Robert and Adam at a fixed time. Otherwise, if we are late, that will signal to them that we've been discovered. They will then leave where they are, and your plan to do whatever you need to do today will probably not happen. We would then be taking Adam and you in different directions away from the City."

"That cannot happen!" I announced. "We have to complete this process in the timeframe allowed us, in the manner that we have told people we've interviewed along the way. I will hurry, even if I have to eat and drink as we dash along."

"That would be better, if you could. In that case, we must run now!"

For over another hour we persisted in our zigzag course until finally we came to a large block of brownstone apartments. I was never sure which cross-streets they were close to. It just seemed we suddenly appeared before them. My having a snack and the juice gave me the added energy to make it. And as we entered an upstairs apartment, to my absolute amazement, there stood Adam, Robert, J.L. and ten huge boxes filled to overflowing with the replies to Adam's questionnaires. They apparently were ones dropped off at the Central Park site or were e-mailed to Eddie's home. All told, we later determined that there were close to 5,000 fully answered with vital information we needed. *(see Appendix "Earth's Accreditation Survey Questionnaire")*

Seeing Adam was such a relief. He promptly asked Robert and J.L. if they had someplace that he and I could lay down for a while. Anticipating our request, J.L. proudly showed us to a bedroom which they had supplied with a bedside table, covered with breakfast snacks and containers of juice and hot water depending on whatever we wanted to drink, and most important of all, a bed.

Thanking and hugging our guides, we closed the bedroom door, ate, drank and slept for the next four hours. We did not awaken until around 11 a.m. But much more refreshed, we dressed, ate and drank some more and finally opened the door into what must have once been the living room and were heartily greeted by all "The Apples". It was time to begin our summation. And we worked nonstop for the next seven and a half hours doing just that.

Five hours were spent going through Adam's questionnaires for his five Standards and alternately discussing my own five. We were shocked at the number of answers to the questionnaires that were in the extreme, either negatively or positively. Very few were checked off in what I would have considered an average or at a normal or more reasonable level. So often, the questions indicating difficult or negative indicators of coping or maturing were answered with "never" or "rarely". And way too many times the questions that indicated comfort within themselves and being at peace with their present circumstances or self-image were also checked off under these same extreme headings. Far too often the questions having a negative connotation, e.g. "Do your feelings/actions harm others?", "Have you become disenchanted?", "Do you welcome change?" or "Are there mistakes you need to ask forgiveness for?" were almost always answered with "frequently" or "always". And most distressing of all were the answers to Adam's questions associated with the Loving Standard. They were so sad for us, and ultimately it got the lowest score of the ten Standards. Too few answered that they did not know if they had been loved or if they knew how to love.

The honesty that these questionnaires represented was especially poignant. Adam admitted that he had gotten some of these same impressions during his personal interviews, but nothing so consistent and plaintive. And the total score for the five Standards of his that we poured over confirmed our impressions. His totals came to 190, and the final tally for mine ended up being 250. The grand total was 440, out of a possible 700.

Breaking down the list of Standards, these were the values we assigned to each one; after spending a total of two and half hours, allotting fifteen minutes discussion per Standard:

Adam's: Behaving Standard: 35 points.
        Caretaking Standard: 40 points.
        Adapting Standard: 50 points.
        Avoiding Mistakes Standard:
                35 points.
        Loving Standard: 30 points.

Mine: Learning Standard: 60 points.
        Remembering Standard:
                55 points.
        Sharing Standard: 35 points.
        Exploring Standard: 60 points.
        Governing Standard: <u>40 points.</u>
           TOTAL: 440 points.

We next had to rank this total figure as to a grade level. Otherwise, it simply was a number within a number, and its significance would be marginalized. As always before with these surveys, we used 10% gradations for determining a letter grade, and then we designated where in the seven age categories that our final total would fall. The grade levels for an "A" were 700-630; "B" 629-560; "C" 559-480; "D" 479-420; and "F" anything below 420. The seven age categories begin at 0-5 years and progress to 6-11 years, 12-19 years, 20-29 years, 30-49 years, etc.

Stunned, we looked at each other in silence after we had completed our numerical assignments to the Standards and gotten the grand total. Never before, on any other world survey, had we come up with such a low score. We double-checked our results, the rationale for each Standard and confirmed that the selection of a given number had been independent of any of the others. There was no bias involved. But the total indicated that this planet had a score of "D-". And it bordered precariously on failing, in which case we would have had to deny further accreditation or occupancy!

Turning to Adam, I asked, "What do we do now? How are we supposed to tell everyone this news? Is it possible we did something wrong in our surveys? You even had questionnaires this time, which was a first. Everything else we did is exactly the same as we did on every other world before this one. What are we to do, Adam?"

"I don't know," he replied, solemnly. "By the total score this world ranks in the lower fourth, age bracket. It's like the entire planet is somewhere between the ages of a 20 and 22 year old individual. In other words, it is borderline adolescence, just barely entering into any stage of maturity. After all these years, this is all they have progressed. I don't know what to say, Eve. Maybe if I take a break and go outside for a few minutes, my head will clear enough to begin to make sense of all this. Do you mind?"

"No. But be careful. Darkness is falling. I think you should still take Robert with you, just to be on the safe side."

"Ok. I'll be back soon. We'll think of something. Don't worry. Love you."

"And I love you, old man."

With that, Adam called out to Robert who was in a back room with the other "Apples", all of them taking a break from their helping us sort through the questionnaires. Without any hesitation, he agreed to accompany Adam outside for an escorted walk. Everyone felt that it would be safer to do so, given the time of day, with daylight fading quickly.

I settled back in a soft sofa, and closed my eyes, as they shut the front door. It had been a harrowing last few days for us, and I just wanted to nap while they were gone. Whatever conclusions we needed to prepare for tomorrow's presentation at St. Patrick's could wait until the impact of our findings was sorted out a bit. We still had a lot more to do to develop that material. I just couldn't believe we had arrived at such a low score.

And then, not three minutes after Adam and Robert closed the apartment door, I heard the two loud, gun shots. And then the screaming…

FIFTEEN: A   PARTING

Rushing to the living room window that looked out onto the street in front of us, while becoming filled with the most intense dread I've ever experienced, I looked down through the low light of dusk and saw two bodies on the sidewalk below us.

Screaming to anyone who could hear me, I shouted, "HURRY!!!   THERE ARE PEOPLE DOWN THERE WHO ARE HURT!!"

Axe immediately ran into the room, yelling, "Those were gunshots.   I just heard them from somewhere below us.   Did anyone leave our apartment?"

"Yes," I acknowledge reluctantly, "Adam and Robert did."

"Oh, no," was all he managed to say.

"Hurry, please hurry," I pleaded.   "I pray it wasn't the two of them who are hurt.   I'll follow you downstairs as quickly as I can.   But, you hurry! And get Eddie and J.L. to go with you.   Maybe there is more trouble building in the area that you'll need help with."

"EDDIE!!   J.L.!!   GET OUT HERE QUICK!! SOMEONE MAY BE BADLY HURT! THERE ARE TWO BODIES ON THE STREET BELOW US! WE NEED TO CHECK OUT WHO THEY ARE AND WHAT'S GOING ON!!! COME ON, HURRY UP!!"

Then the dashing about began. The three men flew past me and scrambled through the dank hallway and down the steep stairwell. As soon as I could put my shoes and overcoat on, I, too, joined them. I wasn't exactly sure which direction to go, once I got outside of their apartment, having been so disoriented when we arrived here earlier that day; but soon enough I saw the meager and poorly lit "EXIT" sign and hurried down the staircase adjacent to it to the first floor and out onto the street.

No sooner had I run onto the stoop and down its well-worn steps, than I was facing all three of our guardians, leaning over the two forms on the sidewalk. There was absolute silence as they did. Pushing them aside in an uncharacteristic manner, I came upon Robert first, his face partially hidden due to his body being partially turned, facing the street. But beside him, lying face up, was Adam. Both had blood coursing its way out of their clothing onto the sidewalk. It was only too obvious; they both had been shot. Rushing around Robert's body, I bent down over Adam and gently lifted his head, cradling it in my arms.

"Adam. It's Eve. Do you hear me?"

A gurgling mumble followed. And while it appeared he was trying to speak to me, I couldn't understand what he was trying to say. It was too garbled. Again, I cried, "Adam! It's Eve! I'm right here. You'll be ok. Help will be coming soon. You'll be ok. Nothing bad will ever happen to you! I WON'T LET IT!!"

And again there were only incoherent sounds coming from him. And by now his breathing was more labored. The clothing over his chest area was becoming soaked in blood. I was becoming frantic. I turned and yelled into the forlorn and vacant street, "SOMEBODY!!... ANYBODY!!!... GET HELP!!! THESE MEN ARE DYING!!!..."

And it was just at that moment it appeared that my screaming had cleared Adam's mind enough to allow him the ability to speak clearly. I was able to understand him, as he turned his head ever-so slightly and said in a low, but distinct voice, "Evie, I'm about There..."

All I had time to say was, "Yes..., my most precious love..., you are. You are going home at last. Please watch for me when you get there. I won't be long, my sweet. Oh, Adam... My most dear and precious, Adam... Ohhh......"

And then he slumped and died in my arms.

In what must have seemed like hours of my cradling him and rocking his limp body, I said nothing. My heart and mind were filling with memories, sights, sounds and events over the countless years we had been together. And I had the deepest, reassuring sense of where his soul was now making its way. At one point I even began to hum one of his favorite melodies. It was as if I was trying to trumpet him home.

But, after this, to the shock of everyone gathered around us by that time, I suddenly raised and turned by head to the heavens and shouted, "IRENE!!! FIND WHO DID THIS!! FIND WHO DIRECTED THIS!!! FIND ALL OF THEM!!! GET WHATEVER HELP YOU NEED TO DO THIS, AND BRING THEM TO ME!!!"

And to the amazement of everyone gathered around me, suddenly there appeared the awesome form of Irene, hovering overhead, looking down on her long-standing friend and companion. She didn't speak to me, but only nodded her head. And in an instant, she was gone. She left no doubt in my mind that whoever devised and planned this plot, along with those who actually committed this crime were now in her cross-hairs. I knew there was no where they could run or hide to escape Irene and her associates.

Then the mournful task of quickly taking Adam's body away from the street began. I couldn't let the authorities take possession of it. J.L. stayed with Robert who also passed away just before Adam. The only consolation I got from Robert's tragic death was that J.L later mentioned that his face was totally peaceful at the end. There was no agony or weariness about him. I knew then that he had also been touched by the Grace-filled and All-knowing Hand.

By now a crowd was building outside, and it made our ability to carry Adam's body even more awkward and urgent. As we entered through the apartment's main doorway, Axe called out to me that none of us could stay in this building any longer. It was clear that all our lives were in mortal danger. "We must leave here right away," he advised solemnly.

I then struggled to asked, "How? We no longer have a reliable car or anything in which to transport Adam. And I'm not leaving him!"

"It's ok," Eddie chimed in. "I know someone who has a van, and he lives just around the corner.

"Can he be trusted?" I burst out, exasperated and progressively becoming overcome with grief.

"I think so," Eddie answered. "I've loaned him my cab many times, and he always returns it faithfully. He never asks questions, nor do I when we borrow from each other."

"Then hurry," I cried. "Is there a back exit we can use now, rather than even returning to the upstairs apartment?"

"Yes," Axe chimed in. "We'll have to go down the flight of steps ahead of you and then go down a long hallway to the alley behind us. And once we get you settled, Eddie and I can come back here and load the van with the boxes of questionnaires. I wouldn't want those to fall into the wrong hands, would you?"

"No," I replied. "We'll have to either find a safe place to store them for the hoped-for, future generations that may follow this one; or if that's not possible, I will have to arrange for them to be destroyed."

"Then, let's hurry," Eddie interrupted. "If you will, Eve, please open the doorway ahead of you; and we'll carry Adam downstairs as gently as possible. While I get the van, Axe, will wind his way back to the apartment and get those blankets you had been using and wrap one of them around Adam."

"Where are we going to go?" I asked as they passed through the doorway going to the basement.

"I have an idea," Eddie answered. "But I'll need to call a good buddy of mine to check it out first. I'll do that after I get the van."

Within ten minutes these two most-trusted friends and companions had securely wrapped Adam's body in the blanket that was given me to keep me warm, and also tried to comfort me as much as the present circumstances would allow. After that was done, Eddie rushed off to arrange for transportation and a hideout.

Axe and I waited nervously. My mounting grief over my terrible loss of Adam was rapidly becoming inconsolable. Just seeing his still, silent body lie covered before me sent me into uncontrollable moments of wailing. All Axe could do was gently pat me on the shoulder as we huddled by the outside door, leading into the desolate alley.

Thirty minutes after leaving us, we both heard someone drive up and shut off the engine. Almost immediately afterward, Eddie opened the basement door and quietly announced, "I have the van, and I believe I've found a very safe place for all of us to hide out until tomorrow afternoon when you give your talk at St. Patrick's."

"Where?!" Axe nearly shouted, beating me by seconds to ask first.

Eddie replied, with some relief in his voice, "My buddy, Zilch, works as a maintenance man and janitor at the Riverside Church, over on Riverside Drive. He gave me the side door, entrance key and instructions on where there is a large storeroom that we can use. It's in the building's basement, adjacent to their large auditorium in that same area. He told me no one else has access to that room nor even has a key to it. He recently had it newly keyed and has not had an opportunity to give anyone else a copy. Even with tomorrow being Sunday, there will not be any danger of someone finding us, he added."

"Then let's hurry," Axe urged. "The longer we stay here, the more likely the danger increases for us, despite what Irene may be doing."

"I wouldn't be underestimating Irene, and whoever she enlists," I interjected, amidst the sweeping grief and anger that was surging through me. "Probably, even now she has arranged some added protection for us."

"Why didn't she provide it for you and Adam before now?" Eddie asked, as he closed the driver's side door and got ready to start the van's engine.

"Because we've always instructed her to

avoid becoming involved in whatever we were doing, unless we gestured or asked for her assistance. We had never experienced such threat or violence before and were unaccustomed as to how we should handle it. But believe me that reticence is over. Now that I have given her free reign to find and bring the guilty ones to me, there is no force that will stop her or whoever else she asks to assist. The Hosts of Heaven have been released to apprehend those who were involved in this crime. They will most likely pronounce judgment and dole out the appropriate punishment for the evil deed that has been committed this night.

"Whereas before, these evil ones' senseless and shameless acts were noted, but repeated they were only censored and issued various, rather harmless sanctions. Or maybe even some stopgap military intervention was committed by various nations to thwart them. But, invariably, these measures always left the masses of people's around this world with the same evil to deal with over and over again. However, because of what has now occurred, the forces of goodness and righteousness for all life have been called to arms. And before this night is over, you will likely be witness to or hear about some long overdue restitution."

Hurriedly, but carefully, the two men placed Adam's lifeless body inside the van, using its rear door entrance. And while doing so, they instructed me to climb into the passenger seat next to the driver. Axe was to ride in the back of the van with Adam to insure that there was no sliding back and forth during our upcoming, circuitous trip over to the church.

Eddie told me he also filled the van with gas in order to ensure they could drive around the city as long as necessary to cover our escape from the apartment. Plus, he hoped this might prevent someone from following us. So once again, Adam and I began a series of weaves and turns, stops and starts, bumps and jolts for the next thirty minutes. It all ended when we pulled up to the 121st Street entrance to Riverside Church.

Even at night you couldn't help but be impressed with the magnificence of this beautiful house of worship. The twin carillon towers rose dizzyingly into the overcast, night sky. And over the next eighteen hours, the regular playing of the bells in these two towers was so comforting to me. It was Axe who told me later that they contained the largest collection of bells in the country. It was the perfect place for me and Adam to be at this time. I knew it was as the night wore on.

As soon as Eddie guided our party into the basement storeroom, both he and Axe told me they had to leave immediately to retrieve the boxes of questionnaires. And, furthermore, after they saw the size of the room, with the extra empty space which could easily accommodate the ten large boxes, they decided they would bring them back here.

Giving each of them a most thankful hug, I bid them a safe trip and emphasized that they had to be extra cautious about not giving our location away. Thankfully, two hours later they reappeared, exhausted but satisfied that they were nearing the completion of the most difficult mission of their lives. The only potential problem during this portion of their retrieving the boxes was when they pulled up to the side entrance to the church to unload the boxes, a New York City police car pulled up beside them. It was only by Eddie telling the officer that the boxes were filled with special, highly personal written confessions from thousands of people for the upcoming Easter Morning service later that morning at the church that the policeman backed off somewhat. However, that was only part of the reason that they didn't get arrested.

Axe sensed at some point the policeman's mood changed completely, almost as if he realized they hadn't mistakenly parked in a "Loading Zone" only. He drove away after apologizing for interrupting their late night labors and said that he felt reassured about their being there was for legitimate reasons. Axe sensed that Irene had someone watching out for them and whoever or whatever it was had probably nudged the officer a bit to move on.

And by midnight all three of us were safely secure in the storeroom, with Adam's blanket-covered body resting beside me. Throughout the time they were gone, the impact of my loss overwhelmed me, and I lost complete control. The tears were unstoppable and my cries echoed throughout the church, I was certain. I couldn't help myself. If someone wanted to find me in those hours when I was alone with Adam, it didn't matter to me anymore. I was inconsolable. It was a wailing that Irene later told me echoed throughout all time and space.

Exhausted by the time my two rescuers returned, we each picked separate areas to bed down until morning. I still had not thought of or even begun any attempt to compose what was supposed to be said at St. Patrick's. Honestly, I had lost any desire to do so. What good would it do? The harm done to Adam by then was frightfully obvious. The dice had been rolled, and this planet offered me scant consolation at that moment. I couldn't think how or what to say to offer any hope or advice for its salvation. It was already in a death spiral.

Sleep came quickly for my two guardians. And blessedly, it eventually came to me as I lay my head on Adam's chest, with my own body covered with our other blanket.

And, honestly, I don't know what time I was aroused, but it had to be sometime after 1 or 2 a.m. It began by way of Irene gently shaking me awake and whispering to me,

"Eve, please, I need you to get up and come with me. Don't worry. I will make sure that you are well rested and prepared for tomorrow's delivery at St. Patrick's. Right now, there is something you need to see and hear... right away. You need to come upstairs to the Sanctuary."

Groggy, but trusting what she asked of me, I gradually became progressively more alert and awake as I rose and quietly followed her out into the basement Auditorium and up a flight of narrow steps that opened into one side of the choir section at the head of the church's nave. Irene asked me to turn slowly and look into the depth of the cavernous chapel. And as I did, I was transformed by the sight before me. Nothing, not anything I had ever seen, would have prepared me for that sight.

Ahead of me was this mammoth space, filled to overflowing with thousands of people; all standing quietly and perfectly still. Before them, on the main floor located just below the pulpits, were two much smaller groups. And assigned or arranged strategically along the aisles and the balcony, clinging to the marble columns and even soaring above the crowd itself were countless forms, all who looked exactly like Irene. Their radiating presence gave the entire void enough ambient light to clearly visualize everyone in the audience. It was a pure white light; not so brilliant that it required you to shade your eyes, but soft enough to prevent you having to squint or turn away. And it illuminated each and every person's face in that crowd before me. None of whom I had ever seen before. They appeared to be wearing the customary dress from every corner of this planet, and their various facial features confirmed it. It was a cross-section of humanity set before me. And they looked absolutely terrified.

"Who are they?" I asked Irene, awestruck and overwhelmed.

"They are all the ones who are responsible

for Adam's death," she replied.

"And now it's time for them to face something they've been able to avoid or prevent from happening for far too long. In fact, I don't know if they would have ever had this opportunity, if my associates and I hadn't intervened after your calling out for me after Adam's death. But, as you can see now, it has been done. We've assembled all the primary culprits and their hired assassins responsible for his death, along with the hundreds of their lieutenants, lackeys and heirs apparent. For the most part, the metastatic drug, terror, financial, business enterprises and the so-called government or tribal leaders of failed nations and their henchmen are all assembled here. And if you will allow me, I probably should begin my brief address to them at this time."

"Certainly," I gasped, unable to absorb to any degree the scope of what was evolving in front of me.

Then, as quickly as one could blink, Irene rose silently about fifteen feet to a position midway between the twin pulpits over the altar railing and suspended herself there effortlessly. It was as if she were being supported by some invisible wire. There was no movement of any kind to keep her elevated. Her wings made no movement whatsoever. It was a glorious sight, even given the tragic event leading up to this moment. And then she spoke.

"I am unsure whether this assembly could have been possible without the urgent plea issued by Eve, who is sitting below and behind me, after the senseless killing of her husband, Adam, tonight here in Manhattan. But what I and all my companions, who are now presently surrounding you and earlier this night made it possible for you to be here in this place, can say at this time is that your reigns of terror and corruption are over. This world can now begin to heave a giant sigh of relief. Nowhere else… anywhere… has there been such a savage and uncontrollable throng of individuals with such violent and worthless intentions and methods. And you've come so near to completely destroying this world. But all that is now over.

"Those of you sitting or standing in this chapel, apart from the few who are standing immediately in front of me, will soon be transported, as effortlessly as you were brought here, back to a region of this world that desperately needs the most vital resource that you can now provide: water. Because each of you has the equivalent of 65-90% water within your tissues, soon that will be extracted for use by the destitute peoples in the draught-plagued areas of Africa. It will essentially be a painless process; almost like getting a vaccination. And after it is completed, finally a suffering segment of this world will benefit from your having lived. Within the time it takes to snap your fingers, you will each be converted into clear, pristine and priceless water. By my estimation, given that there are close to 2,000 of you gathered before me; for your edification, I will provide you the amount of pure water that you will contribute to this thirsty world: 279,000 pounds or 34,875 gallons. At last, some aspect of your having lived will provide the opportunity, however brief, to benefit others.

"But for those of you standing immediately in front of me, your fate is to be much different. You will become frozen in time; able to live without any nourishment, and most importantly, able to be studied endlessly by future generations. You will become laboratory specimens, entities that can be studied, discussed, and even dissected as to how so much evil became so embedded in the cultures and occupations of this world. As science gains better methods of plumbing the depths of peoples' physiology, psychology and motivation, you laboratory rats, will provide more and more insight. You will be forever harmless and mute. And you will help this world to overcome its self-destructive tendencies to become the peaceful and prosperous planet it should have been all along.

"And finally, let me say how almost uncontrollably angry I am about what has happened near here this night. The murderous act that was committed some seven or eight hours ago on the streets of this city was the final evil deed for each of you brought here into this holy place. I can only hope the terror that you are feeling at this moment will be enough to force you in your final, conscious moments to review the sorry state you created for those around you. You no longer deserve to live. Be off with all of you."

And as soon as Irene gave that command,

the immense expanse of the chapel was totally emptied, except for the few individuals standing mutely before her.

"I will find the proper place to house these people over the next few hours," Irene added, as she turned and drifted back down to face me. "And I apologize for the abruptness of what you just witnessed. My anger is somewhat less now that this matter is being tended to, but I must get these other instigators in some kind of secure place before my rage turns on them as well.

"Two things more need to be said. The first is that I will be escorting Adam back Home in just a moment. You are not to be worried about his absence when you get back downstairs. And you will be rejoining him soon enough, as you already must have realized. You're final duty for me is nearly completed. And secondly, you must now return downstairs and get some needed sleep. I will ensure that you do sleep. And you are not to worry about what you are going to say later today in St. Patrick's Cathedral. The words will come to you. Trust me on that. And you should not be surprised that arrangements have been made, for the first time ever or anywhere on the other world's you two have surveyed, for your final summation to be broadcast on every electronic device in use around this world. Everyone everywhere will be able to see and/or hear what you have to say. Unlike on the other worlds, everyone on this one has to hear what is said."

And after all that had happened this next-to-the last day and night on this world, along with my still being overcome with grief over the loss of Adam and then having just heard and seen what she had just done, I only had the strength to ask one question. "Irene, who really are you?"

She turned and smiled at me, answering with, "Wait and see. Like Adam, you will know soon enough. Now, please get some needed rest. Do not be dismayed or overwhelmed by your temporary loss of Adam. You'll be together again soon enough. Believe me."

"I do," was all I could say, as I turned to open the door from the Choir loft and descend into the basement shelter to sleep.

SUNDAY

SIXTEEN: ST. PATRICK'S CATHEDRAL

As promised by Irene, I did find that Adam's blanket-wrapped body was gone by the time I got back to our basement refuge. And by then, my two other associates had been joined by J.L., who was by then also deep asleep. The place had the feel of a welcoming, safe haven. But before I could muster up another impression or thought, I wrapped myself in a blanket and collapsed into a dreamless sleep that lasted until 3 p.m. that same afternoon.

Awakening refreshed and alert, I opened my

eyes to see that the remaining three "Apples" had prepared a hearty, late-afternoon breakfast for me. And it took me only seconds to begin consuming it. It seemed like ages since Adam and I had eaten our last real meal..

"Probably we should begin to head over to St. Patrick's, Mrs. Eve," Eddie suggested, finally breaking the silence of my eating and drinking. "The traffic, even for a Sunday, looks to be heavy. We'll have to take the van, and I'll probably just have to double-park it somewhere in mid-town Manhattan. I'll worry about any tickets or towing issues later. So, if it's ok with you, we need to go now.

"You're right, Eddie," I answered. "I'm not prepared to say much of anything today, unlike the countless other times when Adam and I have shared this duty. I guess it's fortunate that we at least had yesterday to review the questionnaires and determine the final score for our survey."

"What did you come up with?" Axe asked.

"Ahh, you're going to have to wait a bit longer to hear the answer to that question. Even you guys are not to be privy to that, until it is announced to everyone. That's the rule: everyone hears our findings at the same time. Sorry."

"That's ok. I was just curious," Axe acknowledged. "But is it ok if we come inside the church to hear you speak?"

"I wouldn't have it any other way. You've earned the right to be beside me as I speak. Unfortunately, I'm guessing that there is a pulpit of some kind that I'll have to use and that there would be no room for you to stand beside me once I'm on it. But I want you to escort me to it and stand around it as I reveal our findings. And don't be surprised if there are other dignitaries positioned there in the Sanctuary area with us. I have a feeling after last night that, unlike other times when Adam and I did this, now it will be different."

Realizing that our need for extreme caution and secrecy had been addressed by Irene and her hosts overnight, the four of us left Riverside Church calm and resolute. It seemed to me this last week had lasted for years; like last Monday was sometime in the very distant past. But at the same time, it remarkably seemed to me that it was almost yesterday when Adam and I first met in the Eden Garden and then began our lives banned from living in its beauty and security. Time and events can become so warped and repositioned in one's mind; especially when they are associated with life-defining moments. Like in Eden, our time here in New York City, has had a profound impact on our lives. It was here, in this city, that our tangible lives would cease to exist. His already had. And I sensed mine would as well.

Once we drove up to the front entrance of St. Patrick's on Fifth Avenue, it was obvious that we had all been amazingly successful in getting the word out and had given this convocation the right emphasis. The Church was already filling up, with people beginning to stand in the aisles and foyers. Not wanting to cause any commotion, I suggested that we go around to the 43rd Street entrance and try to remain unnoticed as we worked our way around into a room behind and beside the main pulpit. I didn't want to walk a long distance to get to the pulpit, once it was time. This was not a time for me to participate in some kind of a formal processional. And as far as I knew my speaking was the only order of business. No other pageantry or accompaniment had been planned, as far as I could tell.

But I was wrong. Irene had other plans. By 3:30 p.m., we arrived in that little room, which allowed me to be well hidden from view. And within seconds of doing so, the Cathedral's massive pipe organ began playing... much to my surprise. Then J.L., who had been peeking out our cloister's doorway, turned suddenly and whispered emphatically to the rest of us, "It's Irene! She's back and she's brought a bunch of her associates."

Running over to where he was standing, I looked out and sure enough the space between the pulpits, extending down to the Sanctuary railing was filled with others who looked exactly like her. She had apparently taken it upon herself to enlist and transform the Cathedral's organist and bring with her a heavenly choir of voices who began the most astounding sequence of organ recital pieces and choir singing. And it was sometime later that I also learned it was at that exact moment when the simultaneous broadcasting of this service began on every media outlet and electronic device in the world. Most amazingly, unlike when Adam and I announced our results of previous surveys, with this one it was impossible for the audiences to shut off the transmission or turn down the volume. The world was filled with the thrilling voices of this organ and Irene's choir. The time for Adam's and my presentation had come.

At 4 p.m. exactly, or at least by Eddie's watch, I exited our little room and took the ten steps necessary up to the pulpit. I was surprisingly calm as I slowly reached the top of the pulpit and looked out over the massive nave. Every empty space was filled with someone standing, squatting, leaning or sitting. When the organ playing stopped and the choir's singing ceased, the immense area was totally and absolutely silent. There were no coughs, clearing throats, whispering or talking. The area was filled with rapt concentration; Irene had seen to that. It was time for me to begin.

"Good afternoon, morning, evening or night, whichever may be the case wherever this moment finds you, the worldwide members of the viewing or listening audience. And for your information, this service is being broadcast throughout every corner of the world and translated into every language that is spoken, so that all of you can understand what will be said. So please listen carefully.

"My name is Eve. Accompanying me on the recently completed survey of this world was my husband, Adam. But the violence that grips this world found him last night, and he was murdered on a street in this city. He should also be here with me now. In fact, he was to have delivered this summation. His death, like so many millions over the course of time since we were last here amongst you, was so senseless. And it will highlight what I am about to tell you. Every one of you needs to pay close attention to what I am about to report.

"When Adam and I left this world those countless years ago, we were charged with starting other life cycles on other worlds and then much later to begin the process of returning to them to reaccredit them to continue operation. It was a way of evaluating and then saluting them for the progress that had been made since humans began living on each of these many and varied worlds. And proudly, I can report that every other world passed their surveys with outstanding marks. Everyone one of them was given a full accreditation.

"Adam and I came to your world this past Monday to perform your own accreditation survey. We spent the next five days with each of us doing a survey of a particular Standard here in Manhattan. Because of the rich mixture of peoples, institutions and services here, we determined that it best represented this world's accomplishments and progress. Yesterday, we were able to review our findings, study various questionnaires that many of you here filled out and then compiled our summation and conclusions. I will give these to you momentarily. But first I want to give you some impressions that both he and I have about this world. I think you need to hear this from someone who has seen and evaluated countless other worlds... far beyond yours.

"The concentration of power, influence and wealth in the hands of only a very few individuals or groups, almost since the time Adam and I left this world, is absolutely unparalleled in the entire Universe. And the manner in which these individuals or ruling bodies have abused their control over everyone else has left this planet's environmental survivability in grave doubt. Even more distressing to us, they have caused unimaginable harm to its inhabitants, who have suffered unspeakable acts, abuses and privations.

"Time after time, survey after survey, Adam and I have witnessed this over the last week. In short, your world is lost! It may be in a stable orbit around its Sun, but the pathway your world has followed has led you into the densest of woods, marshes and swamps. By now, the ambitions, goals and even daily lives of most of humanity have been so corrupted by the agendas of your so-called leadership that to find your way out of this state will require revolutionary renewal and a staggering commitment to change... by everyone! No patchwork of committee assignments, discussion groups, step-by-step reforms, timid joint ventures or exploratory junkets will even begin to suffice. You haven't the time left.

"In fact, you only have forty years, two generations of time left to get it right. After that, your lease will be cancelled, and your further occupancy denied. Like Adam and I were from

Eden, you will be evicted and banished from this world. In short, you will disappear and all your hopes, promises and dreams will disappear with you; those of you who have dared to have them.

"So what do Adam and I propose as a first step to help you begin to rectify the abominable state you are in? First off, beginning earlier this morning, a modest beginning of this repair process began with the removal of some of your more violent criminals and terrorists. They were rendered harmless. But that is just the beginning.

"And as I speak, a region is now being set aside in the rugged and inhospitable mountains in an area incorporating the countries of Afghanistan, Pakistan, and Tajikistan, and it will become completely enclosed and isolated from the rest of the world. There will be two perimeters around this massive region. One will border the mountain ranges themselves. And the other will be ten miles away from that first barrier. It will set aside, literally, a "no man's land". No one is to ever be allowed in that area or be able to escape from the mountain ranges. And it will be closely guarded and monitored by all the forces of your United Nations. No electronic transmission will be possible either in or out of that area.

"Inside the first fence will be all the individuals who plot, scheme, perform and seduce others with their acts of submission and terror. No women or children will be allowed in this region. And no one will ever be allowed out. But no one will be executed either. Instead, everyone who is placed there will just stay. By doing so, it will ensure the extinction of a rot that has been present far too long in your species.

"I will now explain why Adam and I decided on this dire approach for helping you gain some reasonable control over your lives and future. But first, you should know how we scored the Standards, and what each of them was. However, I will not be supplying you with the actual guidelines we used for the final grade determination. To do so would be like giving you the answers for the Final Examination before you even took the test. But you do need to know what the particular Standards are and the methodology used to arrive at our final grade.

"The Ten Standards, broken down as to which of us surveyed them; for Adam they were Behaving, Caretaking, Adapting, Avoiding/Profiting from Mistakes and Loving; for me they were Learning, Remembering, Sharing, Exploring/Inventiveness and Governing. There were seven grade levels within each Standard, each representing a specific age level: 0-5 years, 6-11 years, 12-19 years, 20-29 years, 30-49 years, 50-64 years and 65 years and over. We assigned ten points to each age level, starting with 10 points for ages 0-5 years, up to 70 points for ages 65 and over. Then we took each Standard and eventually assigned a total numerical value to it, one which we determined you earned through the course of our survey.

"Specifically, your scores for the Ten

Standards were: for Behaving (35); for Caretaking (40); for Adapting (50); for Avoiding Mistakes (35); for Loving (30); for Learning (60); for Remembering (55); for Sharing (35); for Exploring/Inventiveness (60); and finally for Governing (40). The final grade is based on the sum of these scores, which is then compared to the grand total a world could achieve: 700. Next, we determine your standard letter grade, which is based on the usual 10% increments that everyone is used to seeing: 700-630 could be an A+, A or A-, depending on the numerical score finally determined. Likewise, 629-560 could be a B+, B or B-; 559-480 could be a C+, C or C-; 479-420 could be a D+, D or D-; and anything below 419 would be an F, a failing grade.

"Your final score, adding the individual scores of all Ten Standards for this world came to 440. You scored a D- . And if you compare this same 440 with the seven age categories, you find that this places you in the fourth age grouping: at the lower end of the 20-29 year olds. In other words, taken as a whole, your world has the maturity of someone 21-22 years old.

"But don't misunderstand, this doesn't imply that if you scored in the highest percentile that you were geriatric or aged. Nor does it necessarily mean if you scored in the very lowest percentile that you'd necessarily be infantile. But what this final value does represent is the degree of maturity and peaceful coexistence that you have achieved as a world.

"In other words, what this total does mean is that if a world scored in the uppermost level, and most of them did, they were acknowledged as being mature and stable worlds. Neither of these is certainly a classification either Adam or I could assign to yours. Indeed, your world, by this final outcome, can be described quite accurately as being post-adolescence. You have only just entered any semblance of a maturing process.

"And what is so staggering about this is that you've had hundreds, if not thousands of generations to achieve better. You were the first world! What have you done in all these intervening years?!!!

"LOOK AT YOURSELVES, PEOPLE! TIME IS RUNNING OUT!!!!

"And I must now inform you that you are on probation. There is no simple recipe for improving yourselves as a world. Adam and I have tried to help by coming up with a method of minimizing the influence and consequences of having the very worst of you in the public. They can now be locked away and forgotten.

"But being successful as a world is not like baking a batch of Scotches, where you mix certain portions of oatmeal, flour, sugar, baking soda, coconut, extra large raisins and butterscotch chips together, bake so long and you are done. There is no easy-to-read-and-follow-recipe to correcting your shortcomings. To pass the next and your Final Accreditation is straightforward: You must find yourselves! Discover the pathway out of your turmoil and conflicts! Quit wandering about! And for your own sake and for your ultimate survival: Find peace! Find hope! Know true love! Extend it! Give forgiveness! Receive it! Be brave! Be bold!

"One final note. In your favor is the fact that anyone the age of 21-22 is filled with hope for the future and with promise for the course of their life to come. Seize on this hope, make good on the promise of a better life for everyone. Use the energy and determination to be better and to do better. Make this world better than it is. Come out of the darkness. Come into the light. Don't be lost any longer. Adam and I both want that so much for each and every one of you. You are, after all, our children. And we love you dearly. Make us proud. And may God's peace and love, which transcends all understanding, be with you now and forevermore. God bless you all... everywhere. Farewell, my children."

SEVENTEEN: EPILOG

Following the admonition given by me that Sunday afternoon, there were a series of events that quickly unfolded. None were casual nor without awesome significance for me and for the people of this world. And as has been noted elsewhere, by thoughtful and insightful individuals through the ages, once set in motion, even if not appreciated right away, events can cascade in a tumbling fashion… almost overnight.

Banks can fail. Economies go bust. People lose jobs by the score. Changes in the climate become frightful almost overnight. Such was the case over the next few weeks. Earth had been put on notice. Adam's and my Accreditation Summation had not gone unheard or without immediate consequences. He and I never had the opportunity to see what happens when occupancy is on the verge of being denied.

First off, Irene gave me The Apple. She informed me that it was the Highest Authority's way of saying Adam's and my debt had been paid in full. Soon my time would come to join him and the others that we loved and missed so much through all our travels.

Next, I decided to ask Irene if she would see if I could stay a little longer to witness the aftereffects of my warnings and of her and her associates' interventions. It was agreed that I could, but for only a short period. My failing health would be the deciding factor in the time frame allowed for me to stay on.

Confirming events begin to happen throughout the world; beyond those associated with the apparent climactic changes in recent years. It was like the planet was beginning to go silent and deadly still. The winds began to lessen, dense cloud formations became sparse and tidal changes were minimal; it was as if the moon itself was receding. It was like the Universal forces and celestial bodies were beginning to shun Earth; like it had the pox or some other contagion. This world was on the verge of dying, and at last every inhabitant became aware of their need to restore it and them to health and good will.

I stayed on in the same neighborhood where Adam and I performed our last survey. And I was dutifully and faithfully watched over by the remaining "Apples". They sensed that my time was nearing an end. I couldn't stay on to see what the eventual outcome of our Accreditation was. I knew Adam only wished and prayed for the best outcome for everyone on our most precious world, as did I. His sacrifice likely served to bring some final awareness to the planet and perhaps my message that Sunday morning will prompt the needed changes. I could only hope this world would do better for the next Accreditation Survey.

APPENDIX

1. Earth's Accreditation Survey Questionnaire (which was later changed to "'Adam's Apples' Questionnaire")

Please answer the following questions truthfully. No one will EVER know you filled it out. Feel free to explain or clarify anything in the "COMMENTS" section below. Please send it by email to address below, hand it to the individual who gave it to you or place it in a large cardboard box behind the Conservatory Garden in Centi : Park by this coming Friday before 6 p.m. (One ` more of the individuals handing them out will be there to protect them and later properly dispose of them) Thank you for your time and the effort it will take to return it. Your participation and honesty in completing this survey is ABSOLUTELY CRITICAL FOR EVERYONE... EVERYWHERE.

QUESTIONS/ANSWER OPTIONS

<u>STANDARD:</u>   <u>OPTIONS:</u>
NEVER
RARELY
HESITANTLY
FREQUENTLY
ALWAYS

BEHAVING:
  -Do you have goals, dreams or aspirations?
  -Are you achieving any of them?
  -Are you able to cope with daily demands and
      challenges?
  -Do your feelings/actions help others?
  -Do your feelings/actions harm others?
  -What are your goals?

CARETAKING:
  -Do you daily find ways to help others?
  -Do you prefer to be alone?
  -Do you feel isolated?
  -Have you become disenchanted?
  -What have you contributed to others?

ADAPTING:
  -Are you feeling secure?
  -Do you welcome change?

-When should you resist change?
-What in particular do you find difficult adapting to?

AVOIDING/PROFITING FROM MISTAKES:
-Are you in the trial and error stage of decision making?
-Are you able to admit easily to mistakes or poor choices?
-Are there fewer of them?
-Are any, ones you need to ask forgiveness for?
-What are your recent ones?

LOVING:
-Do you love or have you been loved?
-Do you believe you know how to love?
-Could you pass the "Trust Test"?
-What characteristics do you associate with being lovable?
-What characteristics do you associate with being unlovable?

PROVIDE ANY COMMENTS IN THE SPACE BELOW

(E-mail address: adameve@accredit.uni)'

2. CentralPark.com Runners Map[1]
a. Runners Map (Intact View):

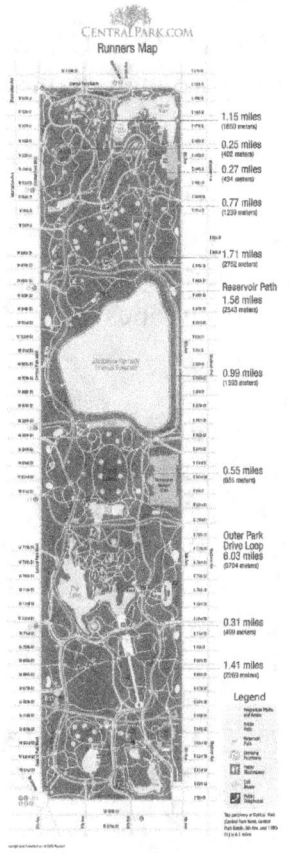

---

[1] Map courtesy of CentralPark.com.

3. Runners Map (Exploded Views):
a. 112th to 102nd Street:

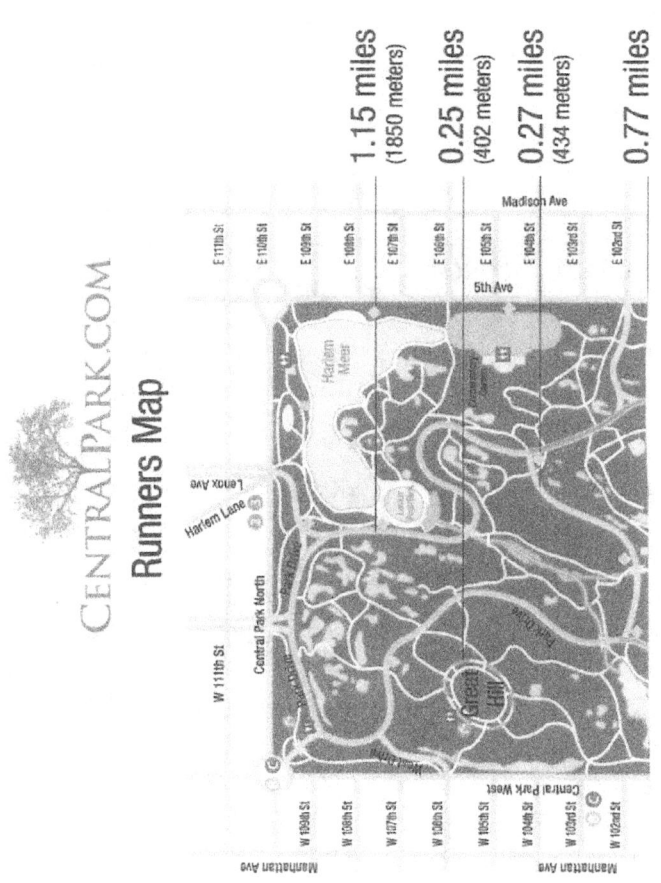

b. 101st to 87th Street:

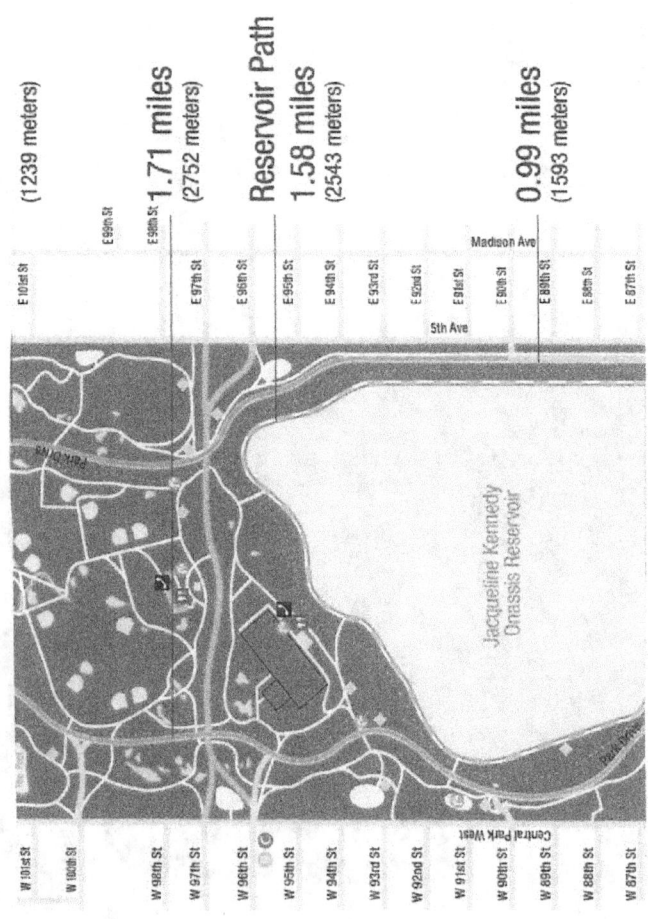

c. 86th to 72nd Street:

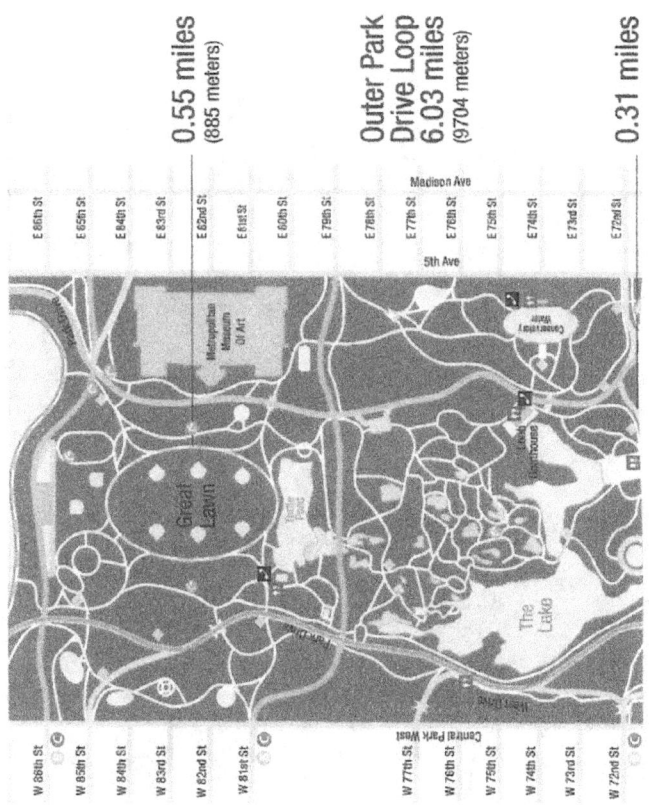

d. 71st to 57th Street:

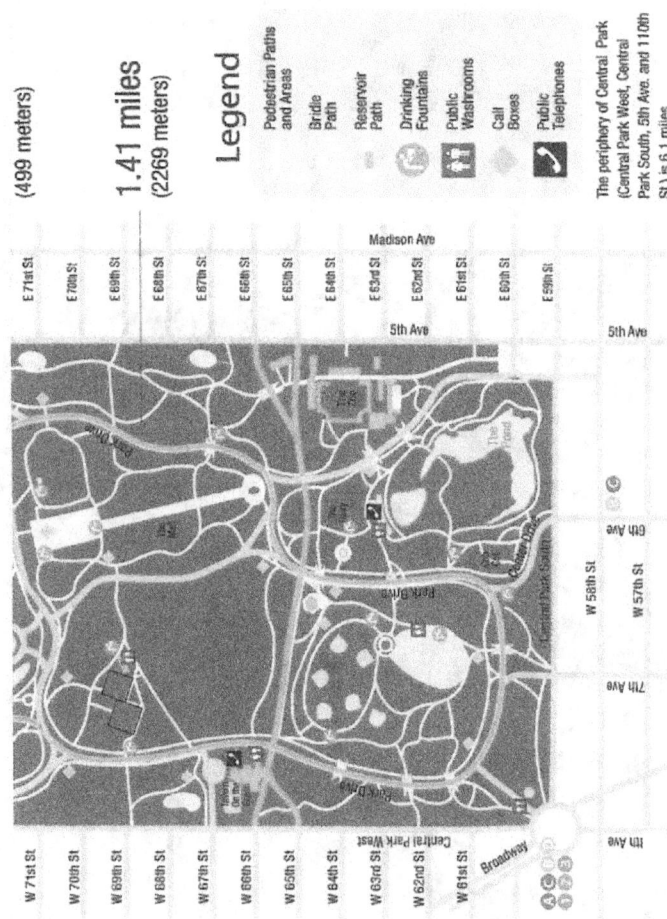

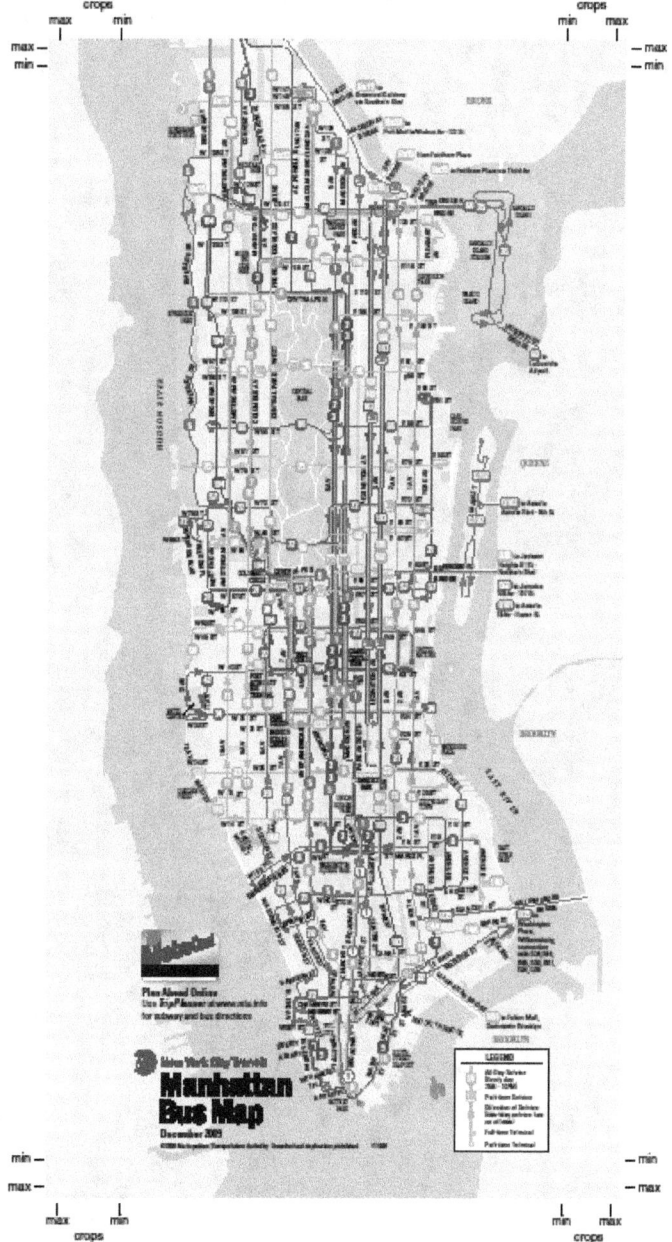

New York City Transit
Manhattan Bus Map

December 2009

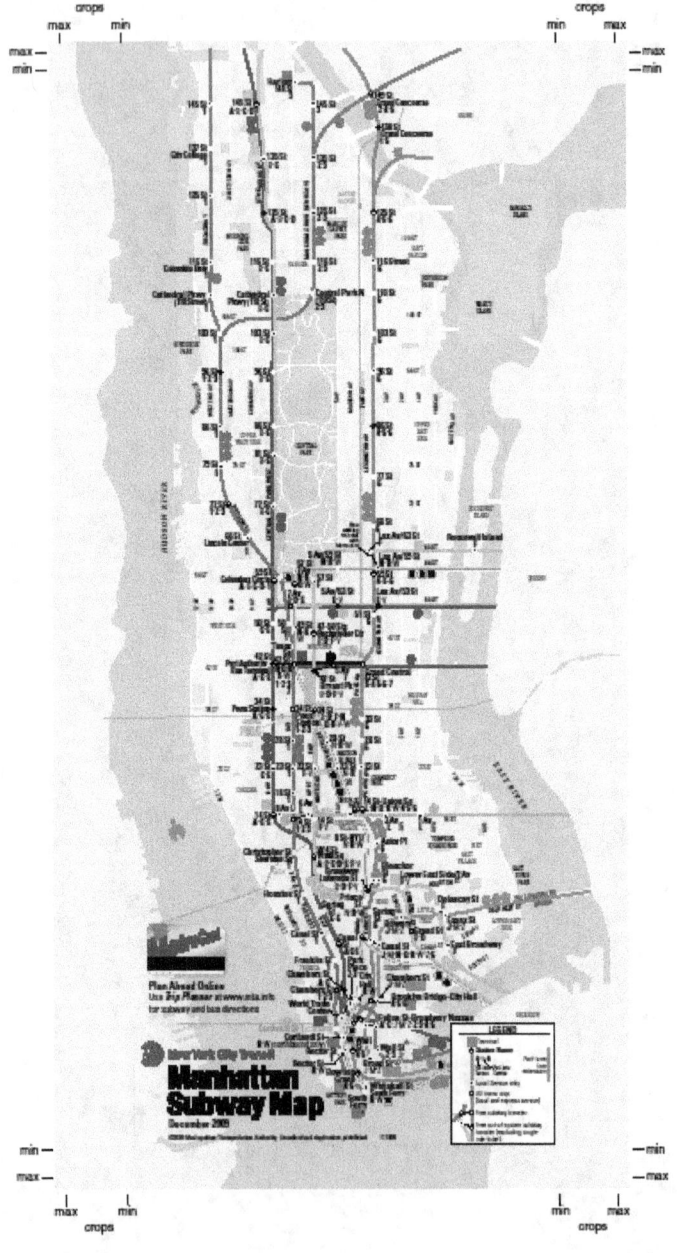

Manhattan Subway Map
December 2009

REFERENCES

1. <u>Class Counts- Education Inequality and the Shrinking Middle Class</u>, Allan Ornstein. Rowman and Littlefield Publishers, Inc. 2007.

2. <u>The Global Class War- How America's Bipartisan Elite Lost Our Future- And What It Will Take To Win It Back</u>, Jeff Faux. John Wiley and Son, Inc. Hoboken, NJ, 2006.

3. <u>Wikipedia, The Free Encyclopedia</u>, "Central Park", "Columbia University", "Rikers Island", "Bellevue Hospital Center", "The Tombs", "Grand Central Station", "St. Patrick's Cathedral", "Riverside Church", "New York Tolerance Center Simon Wiesenthal Center", "American Red Cross", "Calypso", "Islam", "Wall Street", "Intrepid Sea-Air-Space Museum", "Metropolitan Museum of Art", "New York Housing Authority", "Roosevelt Island".

4. <u>The Big Test-The Secret History of the American Meritocracy</u>, Nicholas Lemann. Farrar, Straus and Giroux, New York, 1999.

5. <u>Day of Reckoning- How Hubris, Ideology and Greed Are Tearing America Apart</u>, Patrick J. Buchanan. Thomas Dunne Books, New York, 2007.

6. <u>Superclass: The Global Power Elite and tl e World They Are Making</u>, David Rothkopf. Farra , Straus and Giroux, New York, 2008.

7. <u>The Character of Nations</u>, Angelo Codevilla. Basic Books, New York, 2009.

8. <u>A Problem From Hell- America and the Age of</u>

<u>Genocide</u>, Samantha Power. Basic Books, New York, 2002.

9. <u>Principles of Orchestration</u>, Nikolay Rimsky-Korsakov. General Publishing Co, Ltd, Toronto, Canada, 1964.

10. <u>The Technique of Orchestration, 2nd ed.</u>, Kent Wheeler Kennan. Prentice-Hall, Inc., Englewood Cliffs, NJ, 1970.

11. <u>Orchestration- A Practical Handbook</u>, Joseph Wagner. McGraw-Hill Book Co., Inc., New York, 1959.

12. <u>The Secrets of Songwriting</u>, Susan Tucker. Allworth Press, New York, 2003.

13. <u>The Craft and Business of Songwriting, 3rd ed.</u>, John Braheny. Writers Digest Books, Cincinnati, OH, 2006.

14. <u>Song Man</u>, Will Hodgkinson. Da Capo Press, Cambridge, MA, 2007.

15. <u>The Complete Idiot's Guide to Music Composition</u>, Michael Miller. Alpha Books, New York, 2005.